FALL OF NIGHT

THE TEMPLAR CHRONICLES
BOOK SIX

JOSEPH NASSISE

CHAPTER 1

THE HANDLE OF THE KNIFE that Cade had used to kill his wife, Gabrielle, stared back at him accusingly from the left side of her chest.

He reached out, intending to pull the blade free so he could get on with the rest of what he had to do, but his hands began trembling long before they got close to the handle and he felt a wave of nausea rising up in his throat, threatening to end up on the floor at his feet.

Coward, his conscience sneered. *You did this. She's dead because of you. And now you don't even have the guts to clean up the mess you've made.*

He wanted to curse at it, rail at it, demand that it shut the hell up, but in the end he did nothing more than stand there mutely listening to it because of one simple fact.

His conscience was right.

Gabrielle's death *was* his fault.

There was no getting around it.

Even if he had not wielded the knife that had stolen her last breath and spilled her blood – which he had – he would still be responsible for what happened to her.

The Adversary had played a role, of course. If it hadn't shown up in their house and taken Gabrielle captive all those years ago then who knew where they might be now? But the Adversary *had* entered their lives on that fateful summer day and Cade failed to stop him, failed to protect his beloved bride from the Adversary's vile touch. That, above all else, sealed her fate.

Everything that came after that had been nothing more than the offshoot of that first failure, symptoms of the disease rather than the cause. The years her spirit spent trapped in the Beyond, lingering between the lands of the living and those of the dead, brought there by the very demon that Cade had failed to stop. The Necromancer's theft of her physical form from Cade's own home after Cade had dug her out of the grave, determined to try and put things right. The wards he'd put into place to protect her had not been enough and one of his personal enemies had taken advantage of that fact, had used Gabrielle's body as the cornerstone of a grotesque plan to bring the Adversary back from the infernal realm where Cade had banished him.

But even those terrible acts were eclipsed by what had come next, the Adversary's possession of Gabrielle herself. He had used her body for his own vile purposes while her consciousness was trapped inside her mind, a prisoner of the horrible evil that had taken up refuge throughout her own flesh and blood. Cade couldn't begin to imagine what that must have been like for Gabrielle; he shuddered at the very thought.

In the end, he really hadn't had a choice; even now, in the depths of his grief, he recognized that. To allow the Adversary to continue would have been unconscionable, but he had been all but prepared to do just that when Gabrielle had taken matters into her own hands and had driven the blade Cade had been holding deep into her chest. The magic inherent in the ancient artifact had done the rest.

No, his conscience said. *It was you and your failure that did this. Nothing more and nothing less.*

After it was all over, after the Seven sucked the Adversary from Gabrielle's physical form, Riley and the other knights helped Cade load her body into the back of one of the SUVs that they arrived in. Cade drov straight home and brought his wife into the home they never had the opportunity to share when she was alive, placed her on the table where they might have broken bread together in another time had things been different for them.

And here he was.

He intended to wash her body and prepare her for burial, to honor her in death the way he'd been unable to do in life, but the reality of what he needed to do kept bringing him up short.

"You're running out of time, Williams," he said, the sound of his voice startlingly loud in the otherwise silent kitchen. "Do what needs to be done and then get the hell out of here before the others come looking for you."

He knew the Preceptor and his goons couldn't be too far behind. Once they found Riley and questioned him, it wouldn't be long before they put two and two together and wound up outside his door. It wasn't all that hard to figure out where Cade would go in the aftermath of the death of his wife. Where did anyone go when tragedy struck?

Home, of course.

Johannson would expect him to do the same and for all Cade knew assault teams might already be on their way. He was a fugitive, after all, and not just your average one either. He was an official enemy of the Order, accused of conspiring with a particularly nasty fallen angel known as the Adversary that the Templars had been hunting for years. It wasn't true, of course, far from it, but things had gotten complicated enough that Cade wouldn't be surprised if they shot him on sight and asked questions later.

One side of him actually wouldn't mind going out that way – at least the pain and the misery would be over – but the other side of him refused to allow the Preceptor the satisfaction of knowing he had beaten him. He had other plans for what was to come next but before he could move on to those, he needed to deal with what was right in front of him.

"Now or never, Williams."

Steeling himself, he reached out, grabbed the handle of the knife with one gloved hand and pulled.

The blade came free with a wet sucking sound and Cade knew that he'd be hearing that sound every day and night for the rest of his life.

Gabrielle's heart had long since stopped beating and so nothing but a thin line of blood leaked out of the wound once he pulled the blade free. The weapon felt heavy in his hand and he nearly dropped it as he turned and walked the few steps it took for him to reach the nearby sink. He turned on the water, pretending not to notice his trembling hands in the process, and rinsed the blood off the blade before setting it on the counter.

His conscience had stopped jabbering at him, as if respecting the solemnity of the moment now that he had actively begun the process, and for that he was grateful. He blamed himself for what happened; he didn't need the voice in the back of his head adding to the clamor.

Taking a pair of kitchen shears from the drawer next to the sink, Cade turned back to his wife's body and quickly but efficiently cut her clothing away, pulling the bloody scraps out from underneath her to leave her lying naked on the wooden table that he'd built for her years before. Putting down the shears, he picked up a washcloth he'd set aside earlier, soaked it in warm water, and slowly began the mentally arduous task of cleaning her body for burial.

It was hard, harder then he'd expected in fact, and just five minutes into the task the tears were streaming silently down his face. He knew that his heart would never be whole again.

It was one thing to hold your wife close to you when her flesh was warm and her heart beating powerfully in her chest; it was something entirely different when that heart had ceased to beat and her flesh had grown cold and clammy.

Still he did it, lifting her torso up off the table and holding it steady against his chest so that he could clean her shoulders and back. It was something that needed to be done and Cade had never been one to shy away from his duty to the living or the dead.

Every few minutes he would rinse the towel in the sink, washing away the dirt and the blood that clung to it, and then turn back to the job at hand. His touch was gentle, tender, and if his hands shook a little more than he wanted no one else was there to notice.

When he was finished, he threw the dirty towel in the sink and used a few more to dry Gabrielle's body before lifting it in his arms and carrying it out into the living room where he'd already laid out a sheet from the linen closet upstairs. He placed her on her back in the middle of the sheet, stretching out her limbs so they lay straight alongside her body and brushing the hair back from her face.

Cade stared down at her for several long moments, seeing

everything and nothing at the same time, then bent and gently kissed her pale lips.

"Hold a seat for me, my love," he whispered to her softly. "I'll be there soon."

He took one edge of the sheet and stretched it over her, tucking it in beneath her body. He folded down the top and bottom ends and then wrapped the opposite side around her in the other direction, much like you would when swaddling a newborn baby. He stitched the edge closed with a large needle and a thick length of fishing twine.

More than half-an-hour had passed since he'd started preparing his wife for burial and now that the body was ready he needed to turn his attention to the grave itself. Climbing to his feet he returned to the kitchen and then went out the back door to the yard beyond.

A large elm dominated the left side of the rear yard and it was there, beneath its sheltering boughs that he intended to put Gabrielle to rest one last time. He got a shovel and a pick axe from the tool shed, found a suitable spot in front of the tree, and began digging.

The recent stretch of warm weather had softened up the earth, allowing him to cut through it with the pick axe without much difficulty. After breaking up the topsoil, he switched to the shovel and began the arduous process of digging a hole deep and wide enough for his wife's earthly remains. Thankfully it was pretty much a mindless task and he could let his thoughts drift as he drove the shovel into the dirt, scooped out a load of earth, and threw it into a pile off to one side before repeating the process.

Dig, lift, throw.

Dig, lift, throw.

Don't think about why you are digging this hole or who it is for, just concentrate on the act itself.

Dig, lift, throw.

It took awhile, but eventually the hole was finished.

Stepping back, he leaned on the shaft of his shovel and surveyed the grave in front of him. It was roughly four feet across, six feet long and five and a half, maybe six feet deep. It wasn't perfect – digging graves wasn't exactly in his wheelhouse, after all – but it would do. He knew Gabbi would understand.

He tossed the shovel aside and headed back into the house, its once comfortable silence feeling eerie and strange. Just a few weeks ago he'd been hopeful that the old Connecticut farmhouse would once again resound with his wife's laughter. Now he knew it would forever be as silent as stone. If his heart hadn't already been broken it would have torn asunder at the thought and for just a moment his steps faltered.

Man up, Williams, he demanded of himself. *You aren't done yet.*

He walked into the living room, bent down and picked up his wife's body, and then headed back the way he had come, determined to get this over with before his emotions got the better of him. He crossed the back lawn, stood for a moment staring down into the hole in the ground before him, and then jumped into it with his wife still in his arms. He laid her body down on the bare earth knowing that without the protection afforded by embalmment or a wooden or steel-case coffin, that same earth would reclaim her into its arms just as nature intended. Cade knew his wife would have appreciated that, for she was never one for pomp and circumstance.

Satisfied with her arrangement, Cade climbed out of the

grave, grabbed the handle of the shovel, and began to reverse his effort, doing his best not to look at his wife's shroud-wrapped form as he began refilling the hole he'd just spent the last two hours digging. It went faster in this direction than it had in the other and an hour after he'd started he found himself shoveling the last few clumps of dirt atop the grave.

His arms and back ached, but the job was almost finished.

One thing left to do.

Throwing the shovel down next to the pick axe, he retraced his steps back to the tool shed and disappeared inside only to emerge a few minutes later struggling to pull a dolly containing the headstone he'd painstakingly picked out for his wife in the days after she'd died. Not this time, but the first time.

After he pulled her still-living body from her grave several months ago with his friend, Riley's help, Cade went back to the cemetery the next night and stole the grave marker. He hadn't felt right just leaving it out there over what was by then an empty grave, so he'd stashed it under a tarp in the shed, hoping not to need it again for a few decades at least.

He'd been wrong on that count.

He manhandled the dolly over to the side of the grave and then lowered the stone into place where it belonged. Stepping back, he stared at the inscription carved into the grey New Hampshire granite. There was no name, no dates, just the word BELOVED and a quote from Dickens that she'd remarked upon many years ago.

It is a far, far better rest I go to,
than I have ever known.

Cade ran his fingers over the inscription, feeling the rough cut of the stone against his skin and fervently hoped that this time the sentiment would prove to be true, that she would indeed go to the rest she so righteously deserved. She'd done so much for so many and only the barest handful would ever understand the horrors that she'd rescued the world from through her sacrifice.

Your fault, the voice of his conscience whispered, and he took that as his cue to get on with things. He'd finished what he'd come to do but that didn't mean his work was done.

Far from it.

He returned the dolly and the tools to the shed, locking it behind him more out of habit than anything else for he didn't expect to live long enough to return to this place again, not where he was going. It was time to pay for his failures, time to pay for his sins.

Lord knew there were enough of them, he thought, glancing over at his wife's grave.

This time, thankfully, his conscience remained silent.

He returned to the house just long enough to grab his sword off the kitchen counter where it had been waiting for him to finish his task and then he left the house behind for the last time, stepping off the porch and heading across the yard toward the barn he'd long since converted into his workshop. He unlocked the twin padlocks that secured the double doors and then pushed them open wide. Crossing the threshold, he turned and slammed them shut behind him with a heavy thud of finality.

A few moments passed and then the faint sound of breaking glass could be heard from somewhere deep inside the workshop.

After that, nothing but silence.

CHAPTER 2

THE WOMAN STOOD BEFORE THE mirror, staring at the unfamiliar face that stared back at her from within the glass.

Slowly, tentatively, she reached up and ran her fingers over her face, watching as her reflection did the same. The image looking back at her from the mirror was a decidedly Hispanic one, the features vastly different from those she'd shown the world up to that point but pretty in their own, unique way. This face was wide where hers was narrow, dark-complexioned where hers was almost porcelain white, and her chestnut-colored locks had been replaced by a short weave of raven hair with a cut so choppy it looked like it had gone ten rounds with a lawn mower rather than thirty minutes with a pair of styling shears. She could see the edge of some kind of tattoo snaking up the side of her neck at the edge of her hospital gown, too. The only features she recognized were the eyes staring back at her out of that face, eyes so brilliantly green that she'd once been told that they could make an emerald jealous.

After all that she'd been through she knew she shouldn't be

surprised at this latest development, but this was hitting her harder than most things did.

She was in someone else's body, for heaven's sake!

It was almost too much to believe.

The events of earlier that evening were a bit hazy; she'd awoken disoriented and uncertain of so many things. Who and where she was. How she had gotten there. What had happened to her. All the things that the average person typically used to ground themselves in the here and now without even realizing it had been just beyond her mental reach and she'd been lost as a result, adrift on a sea of confusion that threatened to overwhelm her with every passing moment. Panic had threatened, and she remembered biting her lip to keep from screaming. She fought back the fear with the same grit and determination that had kept her sane throughout her long ordeal with the Adversary. She'd managed to get herself under control, though just barely.

A single thought had been repeating itself over and over again in her mind and she'd murmured the same to the doctor when he finally appeared.

I need to speak to my husband. It's a matter of life and death.

The doctor, Vargas, ignored her rambling, no doubt assuming that she was merely disoriented. She'd just spent the last six months in a coma after all or so he'd told her when he could finally get her to stop demanding to see her husband. A husband she didn't have, according to him.

His pronouncement about her non-existent husband – a husband she vividly remembered - hadn't scared her as much as the realization that he'd been speaking to her the whole time in Spanish.

He'd been speaking to her in Spanish and *she'd understood*

him perfectly.

That was all well and good except for the fact that she didn't speak Spanish.

Not a single word.

She'd stayed quiet after that, allowing the nurse the doctor summoned, an amiable middle-aged woman who wore a rosary and looked at her like she was the second coming of the Blessed Mother, to lead her back to the bed and tuck her in. From that same nurse Gabrielle learned that she was in a private hospital just across the Mexican border in the city of Juarez and that she'd been there for just shy of six months.

Her wristband had the name Anna Rodriguez stamped on it, but it wasn't a name that she recognized.

She waited until the nurse left and then took a peek at the medical records hanging in a rack at the end of her bed. They told her that Anna was a former U.S. Marine who had been vacationing in Mexico when tragedy struck. A motorcycle accident had left her with head injuries so extensive that she'd been in danger of slipping away entirely by the time the ambulance attendants wheeled her into the surgical suite at the hospital. The notes stated that Vargas and his team had gone to work immediately, doing what they could to stop the cranial hemorrhaging and to clear out as much of the damaged tissue as possible before knitting her skull back together. From the x-rays it looked like they'd used enough steel pins and plates that she could probably now set off a metal detector from ten feet away.

The file laid it all out in black and white; so much of her brain tissue was damaged or removed during surgery that there was no hope of her ever leading a normal life if she regained consciousness, which, frankly, no one expected her to do. She'd remained in a coma, lying silently in her bed and being cared for by Dr. Vargas and his staff, until she'd awoken earlier that evening.

Some hand-written notes stated that efforts to get her back to the United States had gone nowhere. She had no living family, no one to take over her care. She'd been away from her adopted family, the Marine Corps, for almost two years and as a result was not a priority in the government's eyes either. Contact had been made with a caseworker in the Veterans Administration, but there was no urgency from that quarter to assume the financial burden of caring for her and so she'd been left in the care of the hospital while the paperwork to bring her home moved slowly through the system.

It was a lot to take in, to say the least.

Especially given the fact that she knew that they were wrong. The body she was in might have belonged to a woman named Anna Rodriquez, but that was not who she was.

Her name was Gabrielle, Gabrielle Williams, and she repeated it to herself over and over again in the darkness of her hospital room to be certain that she didn't forget.

It was immediately apparent to her that her memory was full of holes. She could remember certain things quite vividly – her husband's face; the taste of her favorite ice cream, Rocky Road; the way her staff felt in her hands as she used it to smash a spectre's skull to pieces – but much of what she'd gone through in the last several years was seemingly lost and she had no idea whether that loss was permanent or temporary. Even worse, she had no way of knowing exactly how much was lost, as she had no memory of losing it in the first place!

That scared her.

If she'd simply lost her memory as a result of the accident the way the doctor claimed, she wouldn't be worried. But she knew there was more to it than that.

Much more.

Certain memories shone like beacons in the night, but their very nature made her doubt their veracity for they were more like scenes from some fantastical movie than anything else, visions of strange cities and spectral creatures, of demons awake in the darkness and angels silently guiding their charges through the depths of the night.

One thing was clear, though. She knew that there was a conflict unfolding around her, a rather significant one, in fact, between the forces of good and those of evil, as crazy as that sounded, and, even crazier, she knew that she had a part to play in that conflict. She didn't know all the details, not by a long shot, but she knew that she had come back to deliver a warning. Something calamitous loomed on the horizon, some horrible shift in the balance of things that was certain to effect not just her and her husband but everyone, everywhere, and she was determined to deliver that warning.

Provided she could remember what it was.

She glanced once more into the mirror, taking in the stranger's face that was, for better or worse, now her own and vowed she'd get out of here sooner rather than later.

The clock was ticking, even if she didn't know what it was ticking toward.

CHAPTER 3

ANDALE, ANNA! LO PUEDES HACER. Una pie tras la otra. Empuja, Anna, empuja!"

Gabrielle bit down on the urge to correct the other woman's use of the wrong name for what felt like the hundredth time and   concentrated instead on not falling over from sheer exhaustion as the surface of the treadmill continued its unrelenting movement beneath the soles of her feet. Despite the three weeks that had passed since she'd regained consciousness, she was still struggling to think of herself as Anna. The hospital staff had no problem with it, of course; they didn't know any better. As far as they were concerned, she was the same woman who had arrived in the back of an ambulance just this side of death six months earlier, the same woman they had cared for every day since, the same woman they'd never expected would recover from her injuries.

Anna or not, her sudden awakening had been a bit of a surprise to all involved.

"Dos minutos mas! Andale, Anna!"

Her trainer, Magda, stood nearby but Gabrielle knew from

prior experience that she wouldn't do anything to help her through the grueling session. Magda believed very strongly in the "throw her in and hope she doesn't sink" variety of therapy, something Gabrielle had found out the hard way during their first session when Magda watched her crash ignominiously to the floor when her legs had given out. The hard-nosed physical therapist had stared at her for a moment and then, without a change of expression, told her to stop slacking off and get back to work.

There was no coddling here; that was for certain.

Gabrielle didn't mind. She knew that the clock was ticking; there was only so much time to whip her body into shape and get it ready for what was coming. She needed someone willing to drive her as hard as possible if she was ever going to be ready before the darkness descended upon them all. Magda was all too happy to oblige.

The grueling, unrelenting pace was paying off in spades. Gabrielle's body was transforming itself, regaining the muscle tissue, strength, and dexterity lost at a startling rate during the months she'd lain in a coma. No one had said anything to her yet, but she could tell from the look in their eyes when they watched her that she was healing at an extraordinary rate. Her muscles had deteriorated to next to nothing after spending six months lying unmoving in that bed and yet in just few short weeks she had nearly recovered everything that she had lost. She could feel herself getting stronger every single day and knew her time here was, by necessity, coming to an end.

She'd delayed long enough; it was time to find Cade.

"Done!" Magda called and Gabrielle breathed a sigh of relief.

She caught the towel Magda tossed in her direction,

stumbled off the slowing treadmill and over to a nearby chair, collapsing into it with the grace of a pregnant water buffalo. She didn't care what she looked like. All that mattered was that she'd completed the run. It had been her longest yet; two full miles.

It might not be a Herculean achievement, she thought, *but for a woman who'd been in a coma recently, it wasn't half-bad.*

She wasn't ready to rest on her laurels yet, however. She had a long way to go, given what was to come. Her fitness routine was going to have to continue, even after she left this place.

Her very life might depend on it.

Lost in thought, she barely noticed when Magda came over and sat down in front of her.

"All right. Spill it."

Gabrielle eyed her wearily. "Spill what?"

"Whatever's going on with you," Magda said. "You've been like someone possessed these last few days. I thought you were going to drive that treadmill right through the floor."

For a one crazy, half-filled moment Gabrielle considered telling the truth but she clamped her mouth shut tight against the urge and the danger passed. *She'll learn soon enough,* Gabrielle thought. *They all will.*

She shook her head, both to scatter the thought and to hide her true feelings as she said, "I'm just sick of being helpless. I want to get out of here. Get back to my life, you know?"

To her surprise, Magda nodded sympathetically. "I get it. Really I do. And it's a good sign that you're on your way to healing. But you don't want to injure yourself in the process; that could set you back weeks. So pay attention to your body and don't push yourself too far past your limits. Give it time;

you'll get there."

Time is something I don't have, Gabrielle thought, but she nodded nonetheless.

"Good. Take five and then we'll work your upper body for a bit."

Magda got up to check on another patient, leaving Gabrielle to grab a few minutes of rest and get her breathing back under control. There was a television playing in the corner of the room, set to an afternoon news broadcast, and Gabrielle watched it absently at first, then with increasingly more attention as the nature of the individual stories filtered through her exhaustion. Each segment seemed to be more intense than the one before, each story more violent that the one that preceded it and Gabrielle soon found her gaze glued to the screen with the kind of horrified fascination you feel as you drive by a particularly nasty traffic accident, not wanting to see but unable to look away.

From savage acts of terrorism on the global stage to rioters protesting in the streets in half-a-dozen cities across the U.S., it seemed to Gabrielle that the world was slowly going insane. Every story was filled with violent depravity of one kind or another and as the broadcast went on she began to feel that the anchors were relaying the details with increasing levels of relish, as if taking some kind of strange pleasure in embracing the horror to the nth degree, not wanting their viewers to miss even a single, perverse moment.

Gabrielle was no stranger to violence. The things she'd seen and experienced in the last several years defied most people's imaginations. She should have been inured to what she was seeing on the screen and yet something about it all struck a nerve in the back of her mind and sparked a sudden certainty.

It's starting, she thought.

The thought was a disquieting one, for she wasn't quite sure what she meant. *It was starting? What was starting?* She didn't know. She assumed it had something to do with the Adversary but no matter how hard she thought about it she couldn't come up with any more information. Whatever it was remained locked within the recesses of her memory, perhaps for good.

With that realization came another; she had even less time than she'd expected to get herself back into shape and prepare for...whatever was to come. She'd hoped she'd have a month, perhaps even two, to rebuild her strength and stamina and to regain as much of her admittedly fractured memories as possible, but now she was filled with a sense of urgency, one that suggested her time could be measured in weeks, if not days, instead.

She just hoped it would be enough.

After the commercial, the focus switched from national to local news and Gabrielle took that as her cue to get back to work. She got up, intending to move over to the shoulder press to start her upper body workout as she'd been told, but something the newscaster said caught her attention. She turned to face the screen once more, noting that the male anchor who'd been seated behind the desk in the previous shot had now been replaced by a dark-haired reporter standing outside an older-looking multi-story building with a bright red cross affixed to its side.

Despite the fact that neither the building nor the reporter seemed familiar to her, Gabrielle felt drawn to what was being said and gave it her full attention.

"...that's right, Sebastian," the reporter was saying, no doubt responding to something the anchor had just asked her. "Behind me is the Centro Medico de Especialdades, where the patient they are calling the Miracle Woman of Juarez regained consciousness just a few short weeks ago."

A chill raced up Gabrielle's spine and settled at the base of her skull.

The Miracle Woman of Juarez?

Something about the phrase was oddly disquieting, though Gabrielle didn't quite know why. She moved a few steps closer, hoping it might help her to hear better, but no sooner had she done so that there was a sharp click and the television screen went dark.

"Hey!" Gabrielle said, turning in time to see Magda toss the remote back onto the table from which she'd picked it up. "I was watching that."

Magda looked at her and shrugged. "You don't need to see that. You've got work to do."

Gabrielle's eyes narrowed and she was struck with the distinct impression that her therapist's tone was just a hair too casual. As if she were trying too hard to make her actions seem trivial and unimportant.

She's lying, Gabrielle thought. *I do need to see it.*

She didn't know why, exactly. She just knew that she was right.

"Turn it back on, please," she asked, wanting to see the rest of the segment now more than ever.

Magda ignored her, concentrating on making notes in the folder in her hand instead.

What the hell?

Gabrielle headed across the room, intent on turning the tv back on for herself if Magda wouldn't do it, and she could feel herself mentally getting ready for a confrontation as she went. She wasn't normally the confrontational type; seemed she was wound a bit more tightly than usual.

She better not try to stop me, she thought, and was only slightly relieved when Magda left her alone. Gabrielle snatched the remote off the table and flipped the television back on, but the reporter had already wrapped up the segment and the weather was now on.

Let it go, a voice in the back of her head suggested, but she wasn't willing to listen to it. Not yet.

She whirled around and got right in Magda's face.

"Just what the hell was that about?" she demanded.

CHAPTER 4

ADGA STARED AT HER. "YOU really don't know, do you?"

"Know what?" Gabrielle asked, bewildered by the direction the conversation had taken and annoyed that Magda was being so circumspect about whatever it was. Until now her therapist had always been direct to the point of painfully blunt and it wasn't like her to beat around the bush.

Not like her at all.

The half-irritated, half-pitying expression on the other woman's face wasn't making Gabrielle feel better about the situation either.

Taking a deep breath to keep herself calm, she said, "Why don't you just explain it to me?"

Whatever "it" was.

But Magda shook her head, saying, "It's better if I show you."

Gabrielle stared at her a moment, now thoroughly confused, and then said, "Well, by all means then, show me."

Still wearing that odd little expression, Madga led her out of the room and down the hallway outside. Gabrielle began to slow down as they neared the elevator, but Madga shook her head and pointed at the glowing exit sign at the end of the hall.

"Trust me; if we're seen in that elevator we'll be trapped in seconds. Much better to take the stairs."

Trapped?

Things were getting weirder by the minute, it seemed. Shaking her head, Gabrielle fell in behind Magda as the other woman opened the door to the stairwell and headed downward.

They descended three flights, stopping a few steps from the ground floor. Magda turned and held a finger to her lips, waiting for Gabrielle to nod her understanding, and then, once she had, gestured for her to move closer to the door. Once they were both in position, Magda slowly opened the door, not more than a crack really, just enough to let her companion see into the lobby beyond.

The lobby was literally jam-packed with people. They filled the waiting room chairs, leaned against the walls, and even sat cross-legged on the floor. At center stage were the television news crews, reporters standing with wireless microphones in small circles of light while being filmed by the portable cameras in the hands of their assistants. Gabrielle counted at least four different logos from major networks, as well as half-a-dozen others that she didn't recognize.

Probably local affiliate stations, she thought.

A few police officers and hospital security guards moved among them, doing what they could to keep order in all the chaos.

The majority of people in the room, however, looked like every-day people. Locals, maybe.

A single glance told her that they were from all walks of life; young, old, rich, poor, it didn't seem to matter. They huddled together wherever they could find room, some even resorting to sitting on the laps of those closest to them. Unlike the news crews, who seemed to be in a constant state of activity, the others sat calmly and quietly, patiently waiting for something.

Waiting for what? she wondered, and then, hard on the hells of the first thought, came a second.

What if it's not a what, but a who?

From over her shoulder, Magda confirmed her line of thought without being asked.

"They're waiting for you."

"For me?"

The idea seemed preposterous.

"What the heck for?"

Instead of answering her, Magda inclined her head back toward the mass of people just on the other side of the door. "What do you see?" she asked.

"A whole mess of people," Gabrielle replied.

Magda shook her head. "You're not looking hard enough."

Frowning, Gabrielle turned back and surveyed the room a second time. That's when she noticed that for every two or so healthy people in the room there was a third who was not. Without even turning her head she could see an elderly woman struggling to draw a breath of clean air from an oxygen tank hooked to the side of her wheelchair, a young man cradling the stump of his left arm in his other hand, as if to hide the deformity from those around him, and a young girl, probably no older than six or seven, the bandana tied around her head to hide the fact of her baldness, telling the story of her cancer to anyone who bothered to notice.

It hit Gabrielle like a blow to the chest.

Several of those gathered in the room carried signs asking for help from the Miracle Woman of Juarez, pleading with her to intercede for them in her prayers, to beg God to help them with their particular afflictions. Everywhere Gabrielle looked she saw another hope-filled face betting it all on a complete stranger.

Their show of faith – misplaced though it may have been - was both humbling and frightening at the same time for she had done absolutely nothing to deserve it.

Yes, her being here was a miracle, but it was a kind of miracle altogether different than the one the people believed had taken place. She'd possessed a helpless woman's body, for heaven's sake!

Whatever savior these people were looking for, she certainly wasn't it.

And therein lay the problem.

She had little doubt that if she stepped outside the stairwell, if she showed her face to the people waiting in the lobby, she'd be instantly recognized, and worse, mobbed by those waiting there. The security guards and police would try to maintain order, but in the end it would be little more than a fruitless gesture unless they were willing to use force and that was the last thing Gabrielle wanted to happen.

For a moment she didn't know whether to laugh or to cry.

Without taking her gaze off of the "faithful" assembled out in the lobby, Gabrielle mumbled, "How on earth..."

"Does it matter?" Magda asked. "You woke up when no one expected you to, with no sign whatsoever that you'd been injured in the first place. Even your scars are gone! Someone, somewhere saw that as an answer to prayer, a sign of faith, and suddenly the 'Miracle Woman of Juarez' has been personally blessed by the Virgin Mother and brought back from the verge of death. You've been made whole and now they want you to do the same for them."

Gabrielle turned and stared at her, incredulous. "But I can't do that!"

Magda snorted. "Yeah, no shit."

The anger in Magda's tone brought Gabrielle up short.

"Why do I get the feeling you think this is somehow my fault?" she asked, letting the door to the lobby slide quietly shut as she did so.

Her therapist glared at her for a moment, but when Gabrielle refused to turn away, her expression softened.

"Sorry," she said. "It's not your fault; I know that."

"But?"

Magda shook her head. "No buts." She waved at the door to the lobby. "It's all that fanatical, religious shit. Just gets my goat. No offense but you gotta be a little nuts to believe in all that stuff anyway. Santa Ana? Mi culo!"

There didn't seem to be a lot that Gabrielle to could say to that so she just let it go, but as Madga led the way back up the stairs, Gabrielle found herself thinking that not just Madga but the world was soon going to find out that there might just be a bit more to all that 'angels and demons' stuff than anyone ever imagined if the Adversary had its way.

CHAPTER 5

E XTEND YOUR HANDS IN FRONT of you palms down,
please."
        Without saying anything, Gabrielle did as she was
asked.

"Now I'm going to push down on the backs of your hands
and I want you to resist me while I do so. Don't let me push
your hands down if you can help it, alright?"

A weary sigh threatened to pass her lips, but she suppressed
it and once again did as she was told. She and the doctor had
been doing these very same exercises every day since she'd first
regained consciousness and she could have done them in her
sleep at this point, explanations or not.

"Good. Now turn your hands so your palms face each other,
pinkie fingers aimed at the floor, and resist my efforts to push
them toward each other, okay?"

The two of them went through another half-dozen body
exercises and then out came the doctor's flashlight.

"Follow this with your eyes, please."

Left, right, up, down, in toward her face and then slowly

back out.

"Okay, that's good. Very good, in fact," Vargas said, stepping back. He put the light away in the pocket of his lab coat, picked up Gabrielle's medical file from the bed next to her, and began making notes.

Gabrielle gave him a moment and then asked, "Very good, huh? So that means I can get out of here soon?"

Without looking up from the file the doctor shook his head. "We still have quite a bit more testing to do, I'm afraid. We're going to need at least a few more weeks to get them all scheduled."

This time, Gabrielle couldn't hold back the sigh.

That got the doctor's full attention. Pursing his lips in disapproval, he closed the file folder, looked her in the eye, and said, "These tests are important, Anna, and you really need to take them seriously. We need to make certain that there isn't any long-term damage to your neurological system before releasing you. We don't want you suffering additional injury because we were not quite thorough enough, now do we?"

He's lying.

The thought swam up from somewhere in the back of her mind, as if it had just been sitting there, waiting to surface. As with Madga earlier that afternoon, Gabrielle knew with complete certainty that she was correct. Dr. Vargas was keeping her here for some reason that had nothing to do with her current health or rate of recovery. She could feel it, like a discordant humming way down deep in her bones that made her want to grind her teeth in response.

But why?

She didn't know.

There were no more tests; at least none that needed to be run

28

to determine her overall health or medical stability. They wouldn't be allowing her to push so hard during physical therapy if they were honestly concerned that she might jeopardize her recovery.

There was something else going on here.

The obvious answer, she thought, *was simple greed.* She already knew her case was extraordinary; they weren't calling her the miracle woman of Juarez for nothing. Vargas was clearly trying to understand what had happened to accelerate her healing in so significant a manner and she didn't blame him for that. It was his job, after all, to understand what was going on with the patients under his care. But there was more to it than that. Understanding what was happening was only the first step. No doubt he'd realized the potential implications – both personally and financially – of turning that understanding into a process that could be replicated in other patients. Doing so could potentially be worth millions, perhaps even billions, of dollars over time provided he could figure out a way to claim ownership of the protocol or patent the process needed. The notoriety he would gain by being associated with the discovering the procedure would alone be worth a pretty penny in speaking and appearance fees, she knew.

But something told her that there was even more to it than that.

Maybe it had to do with the cost of her care? It couldn't have been cheap and someone clearly had to pay for it all. Maybe that was Vargas' game; keep running tests, and therefore increasing the cost of her overall care, and then use that as leverage to claim ownership of whatever those tests revealed?

No, that didn't feel right either. While she wouldn't put it past the hospital to pull that kind of nonsense, it felt a little too convoluted. Vargas was up to something else.

Not wanting to raise his suspicions, she smiled and nodded. "You're quite right. The last thing I want to do is jeopardize my recovery."

"That's the spirit, Anna. A positive attitude will only help your progress. And while I hate to bring it up, there is still the issue of your fractured memory. I'm sure you'd like to see some improvement in that as well."

She'd definitely like to see her memory improve, but she really didn't believe that Vargas could help in that regard. She suspected the problem was more a result of her consciousness not being native to the body it was currently in than anything to do with the physical damage Anna had suffered in her accident.

And that wasn't exactly the kind of problem she could discuss with the good doctor even if she trusted him.

Which she didn't.

So she smiled and nodded and did what she could to appear compliant to his suggestions regarding her care while inwardly she was just counting the minutes until the exam was over. When he finally signed off on her chart for the day and took his leave, she breathed a quiet sigh of relief.

Gabrielle wandered over to the window and stared out at the streets of Jaurez below, thinking about her next move. Truth was, if Dr. Vargas had signed off on her release, she wouldn't have known what to do anyway. She knew she had to find her husband and tell him about what the Adversary had done, but after that things got pretty hazy. She remembered her husband's name and what he looked like, but had no idea where he was or how to find him.

And without a computer or cell phone, she couldn't do much even if she did.

She was tempted to ask a nurse for help, but they would no doubt report the request back to Vargas, who in turn would see it as a regression. After all, she'd already admitted that her so-called husband was just a figment of her disorientation upon awakening from her coma. He'd just add more tests to his already lengthy list and that wouldn't help.

Another option might be to bribe one of the orderlies to do some digging on the internet on her behalf, but she didn't have anything to bribe them with, besides her body, and she wasn't that desperate, at least not yet.

For now, she'd simply have to bide her time and hope Dr. Vargas released her soon. Once he had, she could figure out how she was going to track down Cade.

CHAPTER 6

NEARLY FOUR THOUSAND MILES NORTHEAST of Juarez, deep in a tunnel outside of Montpelier, Vermont, Knight Captain Matthew Riley held up a clenched fist, silently signaling those behind him to stop as he knelt to examine the tracks on the floor ahead.

The men of Echo Team's First and Second Squads came to a halt as instructed, taking up defensive positions in a staggered formation along either side of the tunnel, their weapons at the ready and covering their commander while his attention was elsewhere.

The team had been ordered to Vermont earlier in the week after reports of "bipedal, lizard-like creatures in the woods outside of town" had begun to pop up on the dark net, that portion of the internet frequented by hackers, UFO nuts, and, of course, conspiracy freaks. The Order monitored it regularly for just such activity, for while the rest of the world thought such stories were nonsense, the Templars knew better. In between the obviously false stories about the infamous Bat Boy of Indonesia or the real location of the lost island of Atlantis, there were others that contained a glimmer of truth to them, stories that might indicate the presence of paranormal or supernatural elements operating in secret on the fringes of human society. Those were the stories that the Order was most interested in and it had been just such a tale that had promoted Echo's presence in Vermont that evening.

Riley and the rest of Echo Team had set up shop in a local motel, explaining away the weapons in their vehicles as nothing more dangerous than realistic-looking paint-ball replicas when asked by the locals, and then set out in groups of three to search the area in question for any signs of the so-called lizard men.

For the first three days of the search they didn't find a single piece of evidence that there was anything unusual happening in the area. Riley was about to call it quits when Second Squad came upon a set of Croatan tracks. Apparently the lizard people sightings were authentic after all.

Croatan were small, bipedal goblin-like creatures that reminded Riley of a cross between a pissed-off velociraptor and Gollum from the Lord of the Rings. In addition to being ugly, they also had a penchant for human flesh and that meant Echo's mission was far from over.

After that, their luck changed. Within hours of heading into the woods just north of town, Riley and his men ran right into a pack of armed Croatan. He called for their surrender, as the Rule required, only to have his request met with a barrage of stone-tipped arrows heavy enough to force him and the rest of his squad to seek cover. They returned fire, killing several of the creatures in the process, but hadn't been fast enough to prevent the survivors from hightailing it into a nearby cave, which, on closer inspection, turned out to be the mouth of the underground complex of old mining tunnels.

The same tunnels in which the members of Echo Team now found themselves.

Riley was not a happy camper.

For one, he hated tunnels. In his time with the Order he'd been in a couple hundred of the blasted things but he was no more comfortable with them now than he'd been on day one. At 6' 2", he was always having to move through them partially bent over and all that earth and rock so close to the top of his head set his nerves to vibrating something fierce. He wasn't claustrophobic - tight, enclosed spaces in general didn't bother him - just the ones underground apparently.

Like the tunnel he was crouched in now.

To be fair, the tunnel was fairly expansive. It was wide enough to walk three abreast and the ceiling was several inches over his head. It wasn't the size of the place that bothered him, but rather the sense that there were thousands of tons of rock and dirt just hanging over his head. The walls and ceiling were supported by thick wooden timbers every hundred feet or so, but the timbers themselves weren't in the best condition and did little to reassure Riley that the whole place wasn't going to come crashing down around his ears at any second.

He scowled at the tracks that were barely visible in the dust on the tunnel floor. It was too damn dark to see them clearly, given that the only illumination was a faint blue-green sheen coming from the lichen covering the walls on either side. Riley was tempted to use the flashlight on his belt, but he knew the Croatan would be able to see the light from a long way off. Using it would simply give away their position, allowing the enemy time to mount an ambush.

The scaly little bastards.

A bit grumpy tonight, aren't we? an inner voice asked and

Riley could only snort in amusement at his own irritation. The events of the last several weeks, from Cade Williams' arrest to his escape and eventual defeat of the Adversary, had put the entire Order on edge, himself included. Given that Williams was not only an old friend but his former commander and squad mate, the events involving the Adversary were particularly upsetting to him. Cade's subsequent disappearance even more so.

He would rather be out looking for Cade and helping his friend clear his name of the bogus charges trumped up against him than just about anything else, but orders were orders and Riley had been a Templar far too long to simply ignore them without proper cause.

Which leaves me chasing scaly little bastards around in the dark.

He shook his head to clear it of all the extraneous thoughts – wouldn't do to get distracted at this point – and refocuse his attention on what to do next. The tunnel they'd been moving down forked left and right a few feet in front of him. It was hard to see clearly in this dim light, but it looked to him that the tracks continued down both branches.

They split up, he realized.

That left him with two options. Split his team as well – thereby lessening the firepower they could bring to bear in any given situation – or allow one set of Croatan to escape while his entire squad followed the other. Truth be told, he didn't like either option.

For a moment he considered turning around and heading back above ground. He could call in reinforcements and they could give these tunnels a proper scouring.

Of course, the Croatan would be long gone by then. They

wouldn't have entered the caves if they didn't have another way out. They might be small and scaly, but they weren't stupid. By the time he got another squad in here his prey would not only be long gone, but able to come back and harass the good citizens of Montpelier whenever they chose.

No, he thought, *better to keep the pressure on and run at least one of the groups to ground.* If he didn't, he was certain he'd hear about it from those higher up the chain of command and he'd been on their bad side more than enough already.

So, one tunnel or both?

He stared down each passageway one at a time and then made up his mind. He turned, caught the eye of Second squad's commander, Davis, and waved him forward.

"Looks like they split up," he said softly, pointing out the tracks on the floor of both tunnels. "I'm guessing that's what they want us to do as well, which is why we're going to stick together instead. I want your men keeping a watch on our six, just in case the other group decides to double back and try to catch us from behind."

"Roger that," Davis said and slipped back down the line to pass the word to the rest of the men.

When they were ready, they headed out again, moving quietly but deliberately down the right passageway. Fifteen minutes passed with no further sign of the Croatan and Riley was starting to think he'd missed something, a side passage or concealed doorway that their quarry might have slipped through maybe, when something came flying out of the semi-darkness.

Years of battle-trained reflexes were all that saved him; the spear went hurtling past his shoulder as he twisted out of the way at the last second. A quick glance ahead told him what he needed to know; a war party of at least a dozen Croatan were charging down the tunnel toward them with spears pointed in their direction. Others raced along the walls and ceiling with the dexterity of cave spiders, their lizard-like hands and feet adapted across millennia for just that purpose. They would be on them in seconds; if he didn't do something the Croatan were going to turn them all into human pin cushions.

With Davis off to his right and the rest of his men behind him, he wasn't worried about hitting the wrong target so he yelled "Contact!" to warn the others and then Riley pulled the trigger of the Mossberg 590A1 Tactical combat shotgun he was holding.

The boom of the weapon was loud in the confined space of the tunnel; the shot tore through those Croatan unlucky enough to be in the front ranks. The sound was still echoing through the tunnel when first Davis, and then the rest of the squad, cut loose with their HK MP5 submachine guns, firing past Riley's shoulder and into the oncoming party of Croatan.

Their scaly hides were tough, but not tough enough to offer any real protection against the firepower at the Templars' disposal. The Croatan who survived Riley's blast were hit repeatedly, making them appear to dance for a moment in the dim light of the tunnel before dropping to the floor.

Riley shifted his aim, fired again, this time at those scampering along the ceiling of the tunnel, blowing them free of their perches and knocking them down atop the bodies of those below them, causing further havoc in the enemy's ranks.

But the Croatan were taking action as well. Those in the rear of the party, protected initially by those in the front ranks, managed to send a volley of spears and stone-tipped arrows in the Templars' direction, forcing them to lose their aim as they twisted and turned in an effort to avoid being hit. An arrow skimmed off the wall next to Riley and slammed into his shoulder, knocking him back a step. Thankfully the ricochet slowed the arrow down enough that it didn't penetrate the ballistic armor he was wearing beneath his jumpsuit. Some of the other Templars were not as lucky; Riley heard at least two screams of pain from somewhere behind him, evidence that some of his men had been hit. He didn't have time to turn and see who it was, however, for the Croatan were still coming, charging over the bodies of their dead and injured comrades to get to the knights.

The Croatan were so close at this point that when Riley fired his weapon again, the shot didn't have time to spread and the lead Croatan took the full force of it right in the face, blasting it to pieces and spraying the one behind it with a wave of blood, brains, and bone fragments.

Riley jacked the slide again, hoping to get off one more shot before they were completely upon him, but he never got the chance. A thunderous roar filled the tunnel as a section of the wall and ceiling suddenly gave way, cascading down between the two groups, and the ground shook, sending Riley stumbling backward. He held onto his Mossberg tightly, not wanting to lose it in the collapse, as he struggled to stay on his feet.

By the time the shaking stopped, a thick cloud of dirt and dust filled the tunnel making it impossible for him to see anything ahead. He stood there, weapon at the ready, straining his ears to pick up any sound in the space ahead of him, expecting at any moment to have half-a-dozen Croatan come charging out of the dust.

But none came.

Riley waited a few minutes for the dust to settle, just to be sure. When it did he could see that the Croatan were gone, having retreated back the way they had come and taking their dead with them. Riley ordered Davis to check on the men while he stepped forward and examined the pile of debris that now blocked the way forward. He wasn't an engineer, by any stretch of the imagination, but it didn't take much science to understand that one of the supporting beams lining the tunnel wall had collapsed, pulling down a good chunk of the ceiling with it.

Maybe the support beam had been slowly failing for decades. Maybe it had simply chosen that moment to give up the ghost and their presence there at the time was little more than coincidence.

Or maybe the sound of the gunfire had been loud enough to bring it down all on its own.

Could they safely use their weapons down here? Could they defend themselves if the Croatan attacked again or would doing so bring the rest of the tunnel down on top of them when they did?

Riley didn't know and that worried him more than he wanted to admit. For a second time that day he wondered if he'd made the right choice by continuing.

He felt Davis approach him from behind where he'd gone to check on the other men. Riley waited until the other man was close enough and then asked, "Status?"

"Two injured – Hargraves and Stover – but they can move under their own power and should be fine until we can get back to the surface. The bigger issue is Whitmore."

"Whitmore?" The corporal was one of those newly promoted from the regular combat teams to serve with Echo. He was a solid, though uninspiring knight. Good enough when they needed him but little ambition beyond that. "What's he done now?"

"Gone missing."

"What do you mean 'missing'?" Riley didn't wait for an answer. Thinking the corporal might have simply been missed in the dust and the dark, Riley called out, "Sound off!"

The men counted off, one after another, first the command squad, the First and Second squads. Twelve men in all.

But only eleven responses reached his ears.

No Whitmore. Where the hell was he?

He turned to Davis. "Nobody saw anything?"

A quick shake of Davis' head. "He was tail-end Charlie. Grant said he was there when the firing started, but when he turned to check on him following the cave-in, Whitmore was gone."

Not good, Riley knew. The men who served on the Templar fast-action response teams were, for the most part, veterans of the regular combat units. Not the type to go running off into the dark at the first sign of trouble. Whitmore's duty was to guard their six; he wouldn't have abandoned that job voluntarily.

Which meant someone, or something, had forced him to.

It didn't take much to imagine what.

Riley could picture it in his mind's eye. While the squad was distracted by the Croatan attacking from the front, the group that had split off back at the tunnel fork had likely doubled back and attacked from the rear. The cave-in had probably scared the Croatan off.

And it seemed that they'd taken Whitmore with them.

CHAPTER 7

WITH A MAN MISSING AND two men injured, the idea of following the Croatan was immediately discarded. Riley decided instead that they would backtrack along their original course as quickly as possible in the hopes of catching up with the Croatan that he assumed had taken Whitmore.

If he is alive, we'll rescue him, Riley thought. *If he isn't...well, the Croatan will pay for that particular mistake.*

Once apprised of the situation, the men wasted no time moving out. A hundred yards back up the tunnel they found their first bit of evidence that they were on the right track; an empty magazine from Whitmore's MP5. Riley scooped it up and pocketed it for reuse once they got back to the commandery, then continued onward.

Back at the fork, they found evidence of a struggle and a small splash of blood on the nearby wall. On the one hand Riley was pleased to see it – for it meant that Whitmore was still alive – but on the other it was a sign that his captors were not afraid to use force to keep him under their control.

Hang on, Whitmore. We're coming, Riley thought as he waved the team down the tunnel's fork.

# # #

They followed the Croatan tracks and the occasional spots of Whitmore's blood for what felt like hours, but in truth was little more than thirty minutes. The tunnel twisted and turned about itself half-a-dozen times before opening into a large underground chamber.

Riley estimated the space to be about fifty feet in diameter. Rock formations grew up from the floor and down from the ceiling, sometimes meeting in the middle to form thick columns that obstructed the Templar's view and created places for the enemy to hide. A large pile of rocky debris spilled out of an alcove to his right, looking like the remains of an earlier cave-in similar to the one they'd just experienced. On the far side of the room, directly opposite where he now stood, was the entrance to a tunnel leading out of the chamber.

Lying face-down in front of that opening was their missing man, Whitmore.

Resisting the urge to rush over to his fallen comrade, Riley stepped cautiously into the room, moving left as he came out of the passageway, hugging the wall to keep the entire room in view. He signaled to the others, sending half of the group along the opposite wall while the rest moved in behind him.

Riley began working his way forward, carefully checking behind any column that obstructed his view as he headed toward his fallen comrade. He fully expected to find their scaly opponents waiting to jump out and was surprised when they didn't. The rock columns - *Stalagmites? Stalactites? He could never remember which one was which* – seemed like the perfect place for them to hide.

Tracks led from the where the body rested forward, toward the mouth of a tunnel a few yards away. It was too dark for Riley to see very far down the passage; an army of Croatan might be waiting there, ready to charge out at any minute, for all he knew.

Riley signaled for Davis to keep his eye on the tunnel opening, then crossed to his fallen man and then crouched down beside him, feeling with one hand for a pulse.

No joy.

Whitmore was dead.

Riley took a quick glance at the tunnel mouth and then, when he didn't see anything more than he had the first time, laid his shotgun on the ground next to the body. Reaching down with both hands, Riley gently turned the body over.

Whitmore died with an expression of surprise on his face, as if Death sneaked up on him when he wasn't looking. The four-inch slash across the front of his throat explained why. Already weak from his previous injury, Whitmore had probably bled out before he'd even understood what was happening.

Godspeed, Riley thought, as he gently closed the man's eyes.

He lifted Whitmore's right arm, intending to remove the signet ring that every knight wore – the Templar version of dog tags - when a drop of blood dripped onto the floor next to him from somewhere above.

Dark-green Croatan blood.

Riley didn't hesitate. He snatched up his shotgun and rolled onto his back, pointing the weapon upward and firing even before he consciously recognized the shape dropping from the ceiling toward him as one of the largest Croatan he'd ever seen.

The blast from the shotgun caught the creature full in the chest, tearing a hole right through its torso and knocking it far enough to one side that it fell in a heap on the stone floor rather than landing directly atop Riley.

No sooner had it hit the ground than the rest of the Croatan suddenly made their appearance, dropping from the ceiling where they'd been hiding high above, like their now-dead leader. They closed with the Templars lining the sides of the room so quickly that they were among the humans' ranks before any of them had a chance to even get off a single shot.

With the enemy so close, the Templars had no choice but to forgo their firepower in exchange for their swords and within seconds the room was filled with the clash of steel on stone as the men fought back against their assailants.

Having already killed the Croatan that had targeted him as its personal foe, Riley had time to scramble to his feet undeterred, shoving his arm through the shotgun's sling as he did so. He brought the weapon up and tried to find another target, but the enemy was much too close to his own men to allow him to use the scattergun. Frustrated, he let the weapon fall to his side and drew his handgun instead. He was able to get off two shots, killing another Croatan and dropping a third to the ground, before he ran out of targets, the others being too close to his own men for him to risk taking a shot.

He glanced over his shoulder and saw that the tunnel mouth behind them was empty. *If we can assemble there, we can face off against three times their number and restrict the fight to a single front*, Riley thought.

Raising his voice above the din as best he was able, he shouted, "On me, Templars! On me!" and began moving toward the tunnel.

He hadn't taken more than a few steps in that direction, however, when the opening shimmered and then disappeared altogether, the glamour that had created it in the first place dissipating and leaving him staring at a stretch of blank stone wall instead.

For a moment he froze, his mind trying to catch up with the reality of what he was experiencing, and then he whirled about, his gaze going automatically to the entrance on the other side of the room, now their only way out.

As if on cue, a low grinding sound reached his ears and the pile of debris to the right of the entrance began to shift and move of its own accord. Riley stared in fascination as the "rocks" and "dirt" rose off the ground, revealing themselves to be the exoskeleton and flesh of a creature he'd only heard about but never actually seen.

It's a rock troll! An actual, freakin' rock troll!

For a moment, Riley's wonder of the ancient creature overcame his fear.

The troll was humanoid in shape, standing a good eight feet tall if an inch and twice as wide at the shoulders as Riley. Its skin was a grayish-brown color, jagged and rough and reminding the Templar of a piece of unpolished granite. Its eyes were pools of black the size of Riley's fist and when the creature opened its mouth, he could see rows of jagged teeth the size of boar's tusks.

Templar history held only a few records of encounters with such creatures. They were rare and reclusive to begin with, preferring to live deep beneath the surface in the vast underground passages that honeycombed the earth, and only occasionally came into contact with human beings as a result. When they did, though, things didn't usually go well for those who found themselves in the troll's way, for trolls were highly territorial and would fight to protect what they considered theirs.

That thought brought the reality of the situation back to him full bore. Seeing one here, this close to the surface, between him and the only exit made Riley's hair stand on end.

What on earth is it doing here? he wondered. *And how the hell are we going to get past it?*

The troll locked its gaze on Riley, let out an ear-splitting roar that seemed to shake the room around them, and took a lumbering step forward.

Riley brought up his pistol and fired off several shots in rapid succession as he moved forward, but he might as well have been throwing BBs at the massive creature. Its thick hide acted like armor, sending the bullets ricocheting away from it without doing any apparent harm. Riley kept firing, targeting the same general area, hoping the accumulation of damage might allow some of the shots to get through. When the gun clicked empty, he hit the magazine release, letting it fall to the ground as he grabbed another off his belt and shoved that into place in one smooth motion, firing again as soon as it was seated.

The troll responded by tearing off some of the rock formations hanging down from the ceiling and hurling them, one after another, in Riley's direction.

The Templar avoided the first two, dodging out of their path at the last second, but the third hit the ground a few feet in front of him, shattering on impact and sending multiple projectiles in his direction. One caught the side of his head, dazing him for a moment, while another smashed into the hand holding his pistol, knocking it out of his grasp.

Riley staggered back a few steps and shook his head to try and clear it. He glanced around, searching for his handgun, but didn't see it anywhere. With the troll only a few yards away he reluctantly drew his sword.

Gonna have to do this one the old-fashioned way, he thought, and then charged forward.

The troll's bulk would prohibit it from moving quickly, Riley knew, giving him a slight advantage. On the other hand, a single blow from one of the creature's massive fists would probably render him unconscious, if it didn't squish him like a bug outright. He was going to have to get in close enough to deliver a killing blow while at the same time avoiding the creature's greater reach. To that end he ran straight forward rather than hugging the edge of the room as he'd done during his advance, intending to use the rock formations to his advantage as an obstruction to the larger creature.

Unfortunately, the troll had other ideas.

Rather than trying to maneuver around the rock formations, it simply smashed through them with swings of its oversized fists, shattering them into so much rubble. As it drew closer to Riley it lashed out, trying to pulverize him in the same manner.

This wasn't Riley's first rodeo, however. He ducked beneath the swing of that massive arm and then lashed out with his sword, swinging the blade at the exposed edge of the troll's thigh, hoping to cripple it early in the fight to even the odds a bit.

But rather than slicing into the creature's flesh, his sword simply bounced off its hide, jarring Riley's arms so badly that he almost lost his grip on the weapon.

Sonofabitch! he thought, as he scurried back away from the beast. *Just how tough is this thing?*

He was still pondering that question when the troll brought its arm back the other way like it was swinging a scythe, catching him unaware. The blow lifted Riley off his feet and sent him flying through the air a good five feet before he crashed into one of the stone formations and toppled to the ground.

Thankfully, he kept hold of his sword throughout it all.

Riley scrambled to his feet as the troll rushed him, swinging its arms. He parried the creature's blow with the edge of his sword against the inside of its forearm and this time felt the blade bite deep. The troll jerked its arm backward in surprised pain, nearly taking Riley's sword with it. The Templar twisted it free at the last moment, a grin of satisfaction on his face as he understood at last how to injure the massive creature.

Like a turtle with its hard outer shell and soft underbelly, the troll was protected most heavily on the external parts of its body, including its face and chest, and less so on its inside surfaces, like the underside of its arms or the inner portion of its legs. If Riley was going to beat it, he was going to have to get in close.

Very close.

Of course, doing so was much easier said than done. The injury didn't seem to slow the troll down any. In fact, it seemed more determined than ever to smash Riley into the dust. It was all Riley could do to remain standing for the next several minutes as the troll used its arms and legs to smash, stomp, and otherwise try to beat him into the dust. He spent more of his time twisting and dodging away from the troll's attacks than he did setting up any of his own. The few strikes he was able to land left bleeding cuts on the inside of the troll's arms and legs, but at this rate it was going to take him days to wear the creature down enough to land a killing blow.

The troll must have been getting as exasperated as Riley was, for it suddenly changed tactics. Reaching out, it broke off a thick stalagmite growing near it and hurled it Riley's direction but several feet over his head.

Riley was about to laugh at the creature's poor aim when the stalagmite "club" slammed into the ceiling over his head, sending a wave of debris falling down toward him. He had just enough time to throw himself out of the way, taking only a few hard strikes of debris along the length of his body rather than being crushed beneath the rock fall.

The troll rushed forward in a display of surprising dexterity and was at Riley's side in mere seconds. The Templar was still pushing himself up off the ground when the troll raised both arms over its head, hands clasped in a makeshift hammer that was about to land a killing blow.

Fuck me, Riley thought as time seemed to freeze and he realized that the massive creature had, indeed, beaten him. He brought his arms up over his head, instinctively trying to protect himself from the blow that was just beginning its descent, but he knew it wasn't going to be anywhere near enough to save him.

That's when the sound of gunfire erupted around him and the troll recoiled from the impact of multiple semi-automatics firing at it at the same time.

A glance showed Davis and several other members of his squad firing on the troll, distracting it; giving Riley time to get away from the reach of the troll's long arms.

But the Echo Team commander moved closer to the creature instead of getting out of its way. With its arms up over its head, the troll was leaving its side unprotected and Riley had no intention of passing up the opportunity presented to him. He lunged upward with his sword arm extended, driving the blade deep into the soft flesh of the creature's armpit, severing skin, muscle and tendon until it pierced deep into the troll's oversized heart.

Seconds later it collapsed, dead, at Riley's feet.

CHAPTER 8

I T WAS JUST AFTER DUSK when the chopper landed back at the Ravensgate Commandery. Riley waited until the wounded were unloaded and on their way to the infirmary before disembarking himself. After seeing to the rest of his men, he turned, intending to grab a quick shower and then some much deserved rack time, only to find himself facing a squad of four men led by a fifth in the black clothing and white dog collar of a Catholic priest.

"Matthew Riley?" the priest asked, even though it was clear from both his tone and the expression on his face that he knew exactly who he was talking to.

Riley glanced at the red piping around the man's collar, piping that indicated that he was a member of the Holy Office of the Sacred Propagation of the Faith, otherwise known as the Inquisition. Riley knew that his day had just gone from bad to worse.

As in centuries past, the Inquisition existed as a separate office of the Vatican, reporting directly to the Pope. Their days of hunting witches were over – ironically that task now fell to the

Templars – and they operated in much the same way that the Internal Affairs division of a modern police department did; responsible for rooting out corruption and illegal behavior among the thousands of departments and organizations overseen by the Vatican. They weren't very popular, by any stretch of the imagination, but that was neither here nor there in Riley's opinion. Provided they were doing their jobs he didn't have any beef with them.

Then again, he'd never been the focus of their attention.

Davis must have seen the man's rank as well, for Riley felt him stiffen beside him, but he waved his second in command off with a subtle hand signal, not wanting Davis to get involved in whatever hot water he was about to find himself dropped into.

"Yes, I'm Riley," he answered in a weary tone, not wanting to give the men facing him any reason to get excited. Internally his nerves were vibrating like high-tension wires – *just what the hell does the Inquisition want with me?* – but outwardly he was just another tired soldier answering a question from non-frontline personnel.

"My name is Daniels. I have orders to escort you to the council chamber immediately. If you'll follow me?"

"The council chamber?" Riley asked, annoyed at the summons. "On whose authority? If you haven't noticed I just came off a combat mission and need—"

He didn't get any further.

"On Preceptor Johannson's authority," the priest interrupted. "I was told to be sure that you arrive, not what condition you should be in when you do so. Given that, we can do this the easy way or the hard way, it's entirely your choice."

A smile accompanied the threat and for a moment Riley was filled with the urge to smash the man's teeth in just over the general principle of the matter. He didn't like being threatened, least of all by one of Johannson's apparent flunkies, but he knew the guards wouldn't let him get away with cold-cocking the man; they'd be all over him the moment he raised his first. Better to go along with things for now until he knew what this was all about; he could always push back if he needed to later.

If I'm still in a position to push back at that point, the voice of his conscience chimed up, but he ignored it, preferring to believe that things wouldn't get that bad.

"Alright, alright. Cool your jets. No need to get huffy," Riley said. He glanced down at his uniform, stained dark with Croatan blood. "Let me have five minutes to change-"

Again the priest interrupted. "Now means now, Riley. Not five minutes from now."

Riley stared at the man, letting him see his annoyance. Normally that was enough to get most people to back down, given Riley's six foot three inches of height and two hundred seventy-five pounds of solid muscle, but this guy wasn't having any of it. He stood his ground, staring calmly back at the Echo Team's acting commander, as if daring him to lose his temper.

But Riley had been around the block a time or two and he wasn't going to let some rear-echelon yahoo goad him into doing something stupid.

He took a step back and smiled, spreading his hands out in front of him palms up at the same time as if to say, no problem here. "I hear you. Orders are orders, right?" Without waiting for a response, he turned to Davis and said, "See that my gear gets squared away, will you? I'll be down to help with the after-action report as soon as I can."

Davis nodded. "Of course, Knight Captain," he said, stressing Riley's rank, giving him the respect his position deserved, respect the priest had been deliberately ignoring since his arrival.

Davis knew the score and Riley was confident that the other man wouldn't let him disappear into the quagmire that Templar politics had become since Johannson had stepped into the power vacuum left behind in the wake of the Grand Master's sudden illness. If he wasn't back in a reasonable time frame, Riley was confident that Davis would come looking for him and that made his decision to accompany the Inquisitor and his guard detail a little bit easier.

He looked back at the priest and said, "Lead on."

But the other man wasn't finished with his petty display of power. He pointed past Riley's head to the hilt of his sword, jutting up as it did behind his right shoulder.

"You'll need to surrender your sword, first."

Surrender my sword? What the fuck?

A Templar rarely surrendered his weapon and usually only in the gravest of circumstances. To be asked to do so, without any indication of what he'd done wrong or what he was about to face, was a clear insult. Riley knew it, Davis knew it, and the Inquisitor knew it.

Which, of course, is why he's asking, Riley thought.

Refusing to give the other man the satisfaction of seeing him upset, Riley did what he was asked, unbuckling the belts that kept the weapon strapped diagonally across his chest and extending the whole rig toward the priest. Apparently being given a bloodstained weapon covered in dried troll blood wasn't what the man had been expecting, for he grimaced a bit as he handed it over to one of the guards, and Riley smiled a little at the man's obvious discomfort. After that there was nothing else to do but to fall in behind the priest as he turned and headed for the entrance to the commandery, with the guards bringing up the rear.

As they walked, Riley thought about the changes that had come to his beloved Order in the few short weeks since the defeat of the Adversary. It should have been a time for celebration – one of the Templars' foremost enemies had finally been defeated. It turned out to be anything but.

First, Knight Commander Williams had disappeared just a few short days after the Adversary's defeat. Many of the other men believed that Cade left the Order of his own accord, wanting to avoid having to answer for the aid he'd given the Adversary when the fallen angel had possessed his wife, Gabrielle's, body. They never particularly liked Cade and believing that he was a traitor was a damn sight easier than trying to understand what really happened. In some ways Riley didn't blame them; he hadn't believed Cade at first either. But Riley had been there in the end and he, of all people, knew what Cade had sacrificed in order to destroy the Adversary once and for all. Cade would have left the Order, yes, but he wouldn't have vanished. Not without saying goodbye, at least.

But the issue of where Williams had gone was quickly overshadowed when Grand Master Devereaux collapsed unexpectedly during a meeting two days later. Riley suspected the Grand Master had suffered a stroke or a heart attack – he was in his late seventies, after all – but those in the Order's high command were playing their cards close to their vests and hadn't yet released an official statement concerning his condition, so no one really knew. That, of course, had set the rumor mill to running wild with speculation over the cause.

A sudden rash of supernatural activity had kept Echo Team in the field for the last week and a half. Riley hadn't given the situation with Devereaux more than a passing thought during that time, but now he was wondering if perhaps he should have kept his ear to the ground. After all, it hadn't been that long since Knight Commander Williams had been imprisoned by Johannson on suspicion of trying to assassinate the Grand Master. Knowing the charges were false, Riley had helped Cade break out of confinement, an act which ultimately led to the demise of the Adversary. In the aftermath, those in command had been too busy to call him to task for his part in it. Now he was wondering if that particular ballyhoo was coming back to haunt him.

He didn't understand why that would involve a member of the Inquisition, however.

Only one way to find out, I suppose.

His escort led him inside the commandery, up the stairs, and toward the council chambers on the far side of the building. The halls they passed through were unusually empty, making Riley wonder if they had been intentionally cleared. It was still early evening; the halls should have been a hive of activity at this time of night. And if they had been cleared, why? Just what was he headed into?

He glanced at the faces of the men around him, realizing only then that he didn't recognize any of them. That, in and of itself, wasn't all that unusual, for there were thousands of Templars the world over and Riley couldn't possibly know all of them. But he'd been stationed at this particular commandery for nearly a decade and the place was only so big; he knew most of the regulars and even a fair number of the new recruits.

He'd never seen these men before.

Most likely part of Johannson's gorilla squad, he thought sourly.

For years, the Preceptor's security detail had been a position of honor, awarded to those who proved themselves in combat and who excelled in demonstrating the day-to-day virtues held in esteem by the Templar Order. Riley had been asked but never accepted the position – he'd always preferred the action of being on the front line - but that didn't mean he didn't respect those who, like his former squad mate, Sean Duncan, had joined the detail. Duncan would probably still be serving there today in fact if Cade hadn't requested his transfer to the Echo Team in the wake of the attacks on the Order by the Council of Nine the year before.

Preceptor Johannson had been staffing his detail with some of the less savory elements within the Templar hierarchy. Men who, if you asked Riley, seemed more dedicated to following the Preceptor's desires rather than the dictates of the Order. Given the amount of power the seven continental preceptors were granted, the situation had the potential of turning ugly in a big way. All it would take would be one guy with delusions of grandeur and the muscle to back it up...

Riley shook his head, not liking the direction of his thoughts. The Order had persevered for hundreds of years and even with man's seemingly inexhaustible penchant for screwing things up there was no reason to think that anything had changed. If it could survive the egos of men like Beethoven, Jefferson, and Churchill, then it could survive a man like Johannson.

Besides, he thought, *the other Preceptors would never let such a scenario play out. They'd nip any potential rebellion in the bud before it could get out of hand.*

A few moments later Riley and his escort arrived outside the doors to the council chamber. The priest slipped inside, leaving Riley to cool his heels in the hallway with his guards. He took the opportunity to see if he could get any more information about the situation in which he found himself.

"So what's this about anyway?" he asked the guy closest to him.

The guard, a broad-shouldered man nearly as tall as Riley, glanced at him but didn't say anything in reply.

His expression spoke volumes, though; Riley's stomach did a slow roll at the look of disgust the man tossed in his direction.

Riley looked over at the others and found them watching him with similar expressions. One of them turned, spat on the floor behind him, and said something under his breath that sounded to Riley like, "Fucking tailor."

No, not tailor, he realized.

Traitor.

Before he could say anything in turn, the door behind him opened and the Inquisitor reappeared. "The tribunal is ready for you now, Knight Captain," the man said.

Tribunal?

That sour feeling in Riley's gut suddenly got worse.

With no other option but to see what lay in store for him, Riley squared his shoulders and stepped into the room with his head held high.

He immediately saw that a semi-circular platform had been erected at the back of the room, facing a single chair sitting all alone in the center of the room. Seated behind the platform and facing in his direction were three individuals, all of whom he recognized. The first was Johannson, Riley's immediate supervisor and Preceptor of the North American region. The short, dark-skinned man sitting next to him was Colonel Damian Mombasa, commander of the mainline combat units here at Ravensgate. Last but not least was the silver-haired fellow with the permanent scowl sitting to Mombasa's left; Hugh Ochoba, Preceptor of the European region. The three of them had become as thick as thieves in recent months so Riley wasn't surprised to see them here together. What was surprising was the identity of the fourth man standing behind the other three, looking on the proceedings with interest.

Seneschal Colin Ferguson.

What the heck is he doing here?

The Seneschal spent most of his time at Templar headquarters in Roslin, Scotland. It had been there, in fact, that Riley had last seen him a little over two months ago. Someone had tried to assassinate Grand Master Devereaux at the time and Johannson had blamed the attack on Cade, ordering him locked up in solitary confinement in the dungeons beneath Rosslyn Castle until the matter could be investigated further. Riley suspected that Johannson would have been happy to let Cade rot down there and had been trying to figure out a way to get him free when Ferguson had got involved. He helped Riley break Cade free of confinement and provided them both with the means to get out of the country before Johannson caught on to what they'd done.

And now here he was in Connecticut, looking on during a tribunal conducted by Johannson.

Coincidence? I think not.

The only thing that remained to be seen was whether Riley was the star witness or the accused.

Johannson didn't waste any time getting started.

"Step forward, Knight Captain," he said.

Riley did as he was told, crossing the room to stand before the judges' platform. He tried to catch Ferguson's eye, hoping the other man could give him a sense of what was coming, but the Seneschal didn't bother to look in his direction.

Riley wasn't sure if that was a good sign or a bad one.

While he was still trying to puzzle it out, Preceptor Johannson picked up his gavel and banged it three times on its base. He stared coldly down at Riley and let his voice carry for the recorders on the far side of the room to pick it up clearly.

"This tribunal is called to order. Knight Captain Matthew Riley, you are called here today to stand trial for aiding and abetting a known enemy of the Order, namely one Cade Williams, and for allowing that enemy to escape unharmed in the aftermath of a battle in which several of your brethren were killed. Quite possibly by Williams himself. How do you plead?"

Riley stared at the Preceptor for a moment, his eyes narrowing slightly, and then looked at the other two men in turn. It was clear from their expressions that they had most likely already made up their minds regarding his guilt or innocence and he wasn't betting on the latter.

Fuck them, Riley thought.

He stepped forward and in a clear, loud voice for the record replied, "Innocent."

Now all he had to do was prove it.

CHAPTER 9

P LEASE TAKE A SEAT, CAPTAIN," Ochoba said, indicating the chair in front of the platform with his hand.

Riley did as he was told.

As soon as he was seated, Inquisitor Daniels stepped forward and extended a Bible in front of Riley.

The Templar veteran didn't need to be told what to do; he placed his right hand on the book and looked up to meet the Inquisitor's gaze.

"Do you swear before God and before your oath to the Order to tell the truth and nothing but the truth on pain of excommunication and death?"

Lying under oath was not something Riley took lightly and he knew the next several minutes were going to put him to the test, but still he didn't hesitate, knowing that those on the tribunal panel would see if he did and would most certainly use it as evidence of his guilt.

"I do," he said, in a clear and steady voice.

If they weren't too specific with their questioning, he might even be able to keep that promise, even with an Inquisitor asking the questions.

At least now he understood what the man was doing here. It had long been rumored that the Inquisitors were specifically chosen for their ability to discern between truth and falsehood, a gift given to them by the Lord to aid in the Templar mission to protect mankind from the darkness that surrounded them. The Inquisitor's very presence made it clear that the Preceptors were taking this very seriously and that they were hoping to catch Riley in a lie.

Doing so would not only condemn him, but the men who had been with him at the time.

He couldn't afford to let that happen. He was going to have to beat the Inquisitor at his own game, answering truthfully enough to escape detection while at the same time protecting the men who had dared to serve alongside him that night.

One thing was certain; it wasn't going to be easy.

The Inquisitor stepped to the side and handed the Bible to an assistant who had, until that moment, gone unnoticed by Riley. The two men exchanged a few words and then the Inquisitor returned, taking up a position a few feet in front of the tribunal's platform, facing Riley.

The questioning began.

"Please state your name and rank for the record."

"Knight Captain Matthew Riley.""And your current position?"

"Acting commander of the Echo Team."

They went on like that for several minutes, establishing the duties he held, the command structure within the unit, and the like. Riley answered as succinctly as he could, wanting to establish a kind of baseline for his answers so that when he was deliberately short later on, it wouldn't seem unusual.

At last, they got down to the stuff that mattered.

"According to your report, on the night in question you received a tip that former Knight Commander Williams was seen in the vicinity of the abandoned Undercliff Sanatorium, gathered a team, and went to investigate, is that correct?"

"Yes."

And it was correct, *according* to his report, which was the question Daniels had asked, after all.

"Where did the tip come from?"

"I don't know."

That, too, was a safe answer. He didn't know where the tip had come from, for the simple fact that he'd made the tip up for his report and hadn't considered where it was supposed to have originated.

Again the truth, to a certain degree.

The Inquisitor paused, looking down his nose at Riley and frowning as if he'd just smelled something putrid.

"You received a tip and you don't know where that tip came from?"

Riley decided it was time to the rattle his questioner a little. He ignored the look the man was giving him and addressed his response to the tribunal judges, as if the Inquisitor wasn't even there. He knew it would tick the man off, at the very least, and throwing the Inquisitor off his stride emotionally might allow his half-truths to slip past when the time came.

Like now.

"The tip was anonymous; by definition, that means we don't know where it came from."

Inquisitor Daniels stepped in front of him, blocking his view of the judges.

"You acted on an anonymous tip? You expect us to believe that?"

"We act on anonymous tips all the time."

Which was a safe answer, as it was true; they did act on anonymous tips on a regular basis.

Riley didn't miss the glance the Inquisitor gave the judges, nor the signal that Ochoba gave in return to just get on with things.

Johannson was apparently letting Ochoba run the show and Riley had to admit that it was a good tactic. It would prevent him from claiming bias on Johannson's part based on their previous interactions and would make any decision handed down from the tribunal seem to have greater weight. Unfortunately for Johannson, Ochoba was known to have very little patience.

Riley had to resist the urge to smile as his questioner looked flustered for a moment before he got his thoughts in order and changed direction.

"What happened when you and your team arrived at the scene?"

"We discovered Knight Commander Williams in a pitched battle with the Adversary and its allies. Given that I considered the latter more of a threat to the Order than I did Commander Williams, I ordered my men to attack the Adversary and its allies."

The Inquisitor's eyes narrowed as he stared at Riley. "So you admit to intentionally not engaging with Williams, despite the fact he was a wanted fugitive and a designated enemy of the Order?"

Technically, Riley knew they could nail him on that point alone. The Templar Rule, the codified set of instructions and behaviors that all Templars lived by, indicated that a knight was to engage an enemy of the Order where and whenever they were encountered, for they were deemed dangerous enough that their very presence could disrupt the balance between good and evil in the world. In a perfect situation, Riley would have split his forces and attacked both targets at the same time.

Thankfully, this situation had been far from perfect.

"Given the nature of the long-standing order to attack the being known as the Adversary on sight, I determined that it was best to follow the adage that the "enemy of my enemy is my friend." In other words, I took advantage of the fact that the Adversary was already engaged with Knight Commander Williams to open up a second front against the creature."

"Your decision resulted in the deaths of two of your men, didn't it?"

Riley felt his anger rising and fought to control it. He glared at the Inquisitor a moment – long enough to make the man take a step back at the look on Riley's face – and then turned his attention to the judges. Neither Johannson or Ochoba were paying much attention to what was being said; they fully intended to find him guilty, Riley realized. But to his surprise, Mombasa was following the byplay with sharp interest. Anything that concerned the welfare of the men living at Ravensgate was sure to catch his attention and the Inquisitor had all but accused Riley of getting those men killed intentionally. If he could convince Mombasa that he'd acted properly, he might just slip the noose.

A conviction required a unanimous vote, after all.

"We've lost men every single time we've fought the Adversary. Opening up two fronts – one against Commander Williams and one against the Adversary – would most likely have resulted in even more casualties."

The Inquisitor opened his mouth to say something, but Riley spoke over him.

"By choosing the course of action that I did, my team and I were able to defeat those working in conjunction with the Adversary. Yes, two of my men died in the attack; O'Connor took a bullet in the throat, killing him instantly, while Mills succumbed to his injuries before we could get him into surgery. But their sacrifice was not in vain, for it allowed Commander Williams to use the power of the Spear to defeat the Adversary at last."

Riley was about to continue when General Mombasa interrupted.

"Commander Williams was able to activate the Spear? You're certain of that?"

A shiver ran up Riley's spine as he recalled the blasts of arcane power the Spear had produced and how devastating they'd been against the Adversary's human allies. "Yes, I'm sure."

The garrison commander seemed visibly stunned by the news that an enemy of the Order had used a holy relic in a battle, against a fallen angel, no less, and a spark of hope quickened in Riley's chest.

Please let him see the truth, Lord, he thought.

Mombasa didn't say anything further and the questioning continued in a similar vein for another thirty minutes. It was all a big game of cat and mouse, with the Inquisitor trying to force Riley into saying something that would reveal his complicity in Commander Williams' illegal actions. Riley did his best to avoid incriminating himself while still answering each question as truthfully as he could.

Riley's voice was starting to go hoarse from the constant

back and forth when Ochoba abruptly stood. He beckoned for the Inquisitor to approach the platform and spoke to him for several minutes in a voice too low for Riley to hear. From his perspective it looked like the Inquisitor was objecting to something, but Ochoba dismissed his concerns and waved him away.

Turning, he addressed those in the room.

"Earlier we had the opportunity to question those who were present that evening and now we've heard the testimony of Captain Riley himself. I think we have more than enough evidence to come to a conclusion, so I'm formally calling for a vote on the question of Captain Riley's guilt or innocence."

Ochoba looked straight at Riley as he said, "I vote guilty."

Big surprise there, Riley thought.

Ochoba turned to Johannson. "Preceptor?"

Johannson's vote was never in doubt either. "Guilty."

That left only Mombasa, but the fact that the man wouldn't meet his gaze wasn't a good sign. The room seemed to grow several degrees colder as the garrison commander opened his mouth to render judgment.

"Not guilty."

Riley wasn't sure if he'd heard correctly. Apparently, Preceptor Johannson was having the same problem, for he was staring at his colleague in unabashed amazement.

"I'm sorry," Johannson said, "it sounded like you said, 'Not guilty'."

Mombasa rose, glanced at Riley, and then addressed the others. "Yes, that's what I said. Not guilty. And as I do believe that closes these proceedings, I'll take my leave. Good day, gentlemen."

And before anyone could stop him, Mombasa crossed the

room and disappeared out the door, leaving everyone, including Riley, staring in his wake.

CHAPTER 10

A N HOUR LATER THE INTELLIGENCE inhabiting the body of Seneschal Ferguson stood lost in thought in the back of Preceptor Johannson's office as he and his aide went through the day's contact reports, deciding what needed to be dealt with and where Templar resources would be sent the next day.

The trial of Captain Riley had not gone as planned and that failure, small though it was, annoyed the Seneschal greatly. Riley should have been found guilty; Johannson had stacked the deck against him for just that purpose. But, as it turned out, the Preceptor didn't have as tight a reign on those beneath him as he'd led Ferguson to believe and, thanks to rebellion in the ranks, Riley had gone free. Now they were going to have to find some other pretense to remove the Echo Team leader from his command.

Either that or manufacture a situation that generates the same result, Ferguson thought. *Riley is a good soldier but he certainly isn't infallible, as his latest mission illustrates. Maybe all I need to do is give the man some extra rope and let him hang himself.*

He had been working to destabilize the Templar Order from within for some time now and those efforts were finally reaching a critical phase. Men like Riley, and Williams before him, were a nuisance, nothing more, but he'd just as soon have them out of the way before the final push to subvert the Order got underway along with the rest of his plan.

It seemed the old adage was true; if he wanted it done right, he was going to have to do it himself.

He was pondering how he might carry that out when something Johannson's aide said brought him out of his reverie. He turned, focusing his attention back on the other two men just as the Preceptor asked his aide to repeat himself.

"They're calling her the Miracle Woman of Juarez, sir."

Johannson sniffed the air and looked at the aide as if the man had stepped in a pile of dog shit and then tracked it into the office behind him. "Who in heaven's name is that? And why should I care?"

To his credit, the aide didn't flinch at the Preceptor's tone. Perhaps he'd long grown used to it. Instead, he simply answered the man's question.

"Three weeks ago a woman with a severe head injury woke up after spending considerable time in a coma. The doctor who treated her has publically stated that he never expected her to regain consciousness given the extensive damage she suffered. He has, in fact, insisted that it was physically impossible for her to do so. Not only did she wake up, but she is fully functional and has no physical signs that she had been injured in the first place. The damage to her skull and the scars left behind by the extensive surgery that was used to keep her alive have all vanished. The locals are convinced that she's been healed by the hand of God."

Johannson sighed. "We get a thousand reports of such "miraculous healings" in any given month. What gives this one any more relevance than any of the others?"

For the first time since entering the room, the aide looked uncomfortable. He hesitated, trying to find a way to answer the question without angering the Preceptor only to end up doing just that with his delay.

"Out with it, man. Don't just stand there!"

"Yes, sir. When the woman first awoke, she apparently asked to see her husband."

Johannson scowled. "So?"

"The man she asked for, the man she claims is her husband, is named Cade Williams."

"Coincidence, no more," Johansson said, but Ferguson wasn't sure. His intuition was practically screaming at him to pay attention and he'd learned to trust it. There was something important about this "miracle woman," it was saying, something that could have unexpected consequences on his plans for the future. He needed to deal with it now before things got out of hand.

Johannson had already decided otherwise, however. "Mark it as reviewed and file it with the rest of..."

Ferguson interrupted. "If I may, Preceptor?"

The other man turned to face him. "Of course, Seneschal," Johannson said, trying to curry favor as always.

Ferguson turned and addressed the aide. "Just how reliable is the source of this information?"

"We have automated systems that monitor various databases for specific keyword triggers, Seneschal. Knight Commander Williams' name was added to that trigger list several months ago at Preceptor Johannson's request. This alert was spawned from that automated system."

Ferguson nodded as if he were well aware of the information he'd just been given, when in reality it was all new to him. The real Ferguson would most likely have known it, but he was not that man. Still, appearances must be kept up and all that. He would reveal himself when it was time to do so and not a second before.

"Yes, I understand how it was obtained," he said to the aide. "What I'm asking about is the reliability of the information itself. How do you know that the Cade Williams this woman is referring to is, in fact, the Cade Williams that was until recently a member of this Order?"

"We don't," the aide replied without hesitation. "Not with any certainty, at least. There are one hundred and eight other Cade Williams living in North America and the woman could have been referring to any one of them, I suppose."

"And yet it struck you as important enough to bring to the Preceptor. Why is that?"

For the first time the aide looked decidedly uncomfortable as he said, "It just didn't...feel right, Seneschal."

Ferguson stared at the man. "It didn't *feel* right?"

The aide nodded, though none too eagerly. Apparently telling the Order's second-most senior officer that he was acting on little more than gut instinct wasn't something he was all that proud of.

"When the report crossed my desk, I felt it was...important. Like there was more to the story than what was contained in the report and that it was worth looking into given the Preceptor's interest in former Commander Williams."

Ferguson didn't say anything, just continued to stare at the man as his considered his next move. Inwardly he was impressed with the man's intuition, for his own was telling him the exact same thing, but didn't want to call any more attention to the issue.

Mistaking his silence for disapproval, the aide began to apologize.

"I'm sorry," he said, looking first at the Seneschal and then over at the Preceptor as he went on. "I shouldn't have been so hasty in bringing this to your attention. I will gather more information..."

Ferguson shook his head, cutting the man off. "No, you did the right thing. I'm inclined to agree with you; this needs further investigation."

"It does?" the Preceptor asked, surprised by the Seneschal's interest.

"Yes, it does. Might I suggest the young Inquisitor from the tribunal this morning?"

Johannson frowned. "Daniels? Suggest him for what?"

"To investigate this 'miracle woman' situation," Ferguson said. "Provided, of course, you agree that it bears looking into?"

"If you think it will be..."

Ferguson cut him off. "I do. Please see to it. And send Inquisitor Daniels to my office. I'd like to have a word with him before he leaves."

"Of course, Seneschal," Johannson replied.

Perhaps this day could be salvaged after all, Ferguson thought, as he took his leave of the two men, his thoughts already on the meeting to come.

If the miracle woman of Juarez was who he thought she was, she was in for a bit of a surprise.

# # #

An hour later there was a knock on the door of the office that had been assigned to the Seneschal upon his arrival at the commandery several weeks ago.

"Come!" he called.

The door opened, admitting the Inquisitor from the tribunal. He was dressed as a Catholic priest, the white of his dog collar standing out in sharp relief against his black pants, shirt, and shoes.

"You asked to see me, Seneschal?"

"I did, Daniels. Please take a seat," Ferguson said, gesturing at one of the two chairs in front of his desk. He waited until the other man had done so, then went on.

"First, thank you for your efforts this morning. You did well."

Daniels shook his head, but didn't say anything.

The Seneschal didn't need an Inquisitor's discernment to know Daniels thought he'd failed to do his duty with regard to Knight Captain Riley, but frankly, he didn't care how the man felt either way. He needed a tool to carry out the assignment ahead of them and Daniels was as good a tool as any.

Still, Ferguson couldn't help but smile inwardly at the knowledge that he'd chosen a man who had both personal integrity and dedication to the Order. It made what was to come all the sweeter.

"I understand you might be disappointed in the end result, but as far as I'm concerned that doesn't reflect on the way you handled yourself in a difficult situation. In fact, it's precisely why I've chosen you for this assignment."

Daniels looked up, a bit of interest in his eyes now.

"Assignment?"

"Yes. We've had reports of a supposed miracle taking place in Juarez, Mexico. A woman who suffered severe trauma has emerged from a coma with no sign of her injuries or the subsequent surgeries she underwent to save her life. It is as if she had never been injured in the first place. I want you to look into whatever is going on there and determine the truth by the miracle claims."

"Of course, Seneschal. I'll leave immediately."

Ferguson smiled. "That's what I like to see; devotion to duty. Come, let us pray for your success."

The Seneschal rose and moved to stand beneath a large cross hanging on one wall. The Inquisitor came over and knelt down in front of him, head bowed.

Ferguson rested his hands on either side of the man's head.

"Heavenly Father," he began but went no further. Before the Inquisitor could understand what was happening, the Seneschal slipped one hand around the back of the man's head and used the other to grab him by the chin. Quick as a striking snake he wrenched his hands in opposite directions, snapping the Inquisitor's neck and killing him instantly.

Ferguson let the body fall to the floor and then extended his hands over it, palms down. He began chanting a phrase over and over again in a deep, guttural tongue that the human throat had never been designed to handle. The words reverberated through the room in a way that normal speech did not, digging deep into structure around him, breaking down the barriers that protected this world from the next, reaching out into the mists and darkness beyond, a beacon calling forth a very particular servant to fill his need. The lights in the room dimmed, the shadows growing darker, stronger, and still Ferguson continued, calling, seeking, summoning that which he wanted, until with a snap of power like breaking of a high tension wire something else suddenly stood in the room with him.

In this human form he couldn't see it clearly, just a suggestion of a dark humanoid shape covered with spikes that jutted out in every direction standing there in the shadows of the room, but he knew it for what it was. He had once commanded legions of the same and fully intended to do so again, but for right now all he needed was this single servitor demon to carry out his desires.

He let his power flair for a moment, to keep the creature from mistaking who it was dealing with, and then, when he was certain he had the demon's attention, gestured at the body lying on the floor.

Without hesitation the servitor demon flowed across the floor and settled over the form of the dead Inquisitor. Ferguson watched as the darkness spread out across the dead man's flesh and then seeped down into it, disappearing from view. Seconds later the Inquisitor's eyes popped open, roaming in their sockets for a moment before coming to rest on Ferguson where he stood looking down.

The former Inquisitor opened his mouth a couple times, like a fish out of water, as it sought to gain control of the body's vocal chords. Finally it managed to gasp out one word.

"Master."

Ferguson nodded. "I have a special job for you," he said and then reached down to help the now living dead man to his feet.

CHAPTER 11

A SHARP NOISE FROM OUT in the corridor woke Gabrielle shortly after midnight. She lay in bed for a time trying to figure out what the sound had been, but when it wasn't repeated she tried to get back to sleep.

Unfortunately, it wasn't that easy.

After thrashing about for another half-hour she finally rose and got out of bed, intending to take a short walk around the unit in the hopes of tiring herself out enough to sleep for the rest of the night. The tiled floor was cool beneath her feet and the hospital gown she wore was by no means draft proof, but it was late, the halls were most likely empty, and she didn't think anyone would notice her less-than-appropriate attire.

Out in the corridor it was dark, with just a few lights on here and there along the hallway and a brighter cone of light illuminating the nursing station with two women sitting at the far end. Not wanting to talk to anyone, Gabrielle turned and headed in the opposite direction, her arms crossed in front of her chest to ward off the chill of the night air.

The hospital was set up in a square surrounding a central

courtyard and she was three-quarters of the way around the circuit, moving nearly silently through the darkness with only the light of the moon coming in through the occasional window to guide her way when she saw a crescent of light spilling from a partially open door and heard a male voice speaking angrily from somewhere inside the room.

If she'd been asked later, she wouldn't have been able to put into words just what caught her attention and made her creep quietly forward in order to listen more closely to what was being said instead of passing by. Truth was it was more a feeling than anything else, a sudden sense that there was something going on, something wrong, and it would be in her best interest to find out what. Her instincts were screaming at her to pay attention and so that's what she did.

A glance up and down the hall to be sure she wasn't being observed and then she settled against the wall a few feet from the door. She closed her eyes, trying to focus in on the man's voice so she could hear what was being said.

"...I hope so. I've been trying to reach Agent Robertson for the last ten minutes but I keep getting put on hold," the speaker said and with just those few words Gabrielle recognized him as Dr. Vargas. "Is he in or not?"

Agent Robertson? Who on earth was that?

The operator must have finally found Robertson because Vargas suddenly started talking again.

"This is Dr. Raul Vargas, at Centro Medico de Especialdades in Jaurez, Mexico. You told me to call if I encountered anything unusual."

The man on the other end of the line must have encouraged Vargas to continue for he said, "I've got an Hispanic female in my trauma unit who just woke up from a six-month coma as if she was never in it in the first place. Her body is healing at a prodigious rate and her brain activity seems to be off the charts. She was a practically a vegetable a couple of weeks ago and now she's not only up and walking around but performing physical activities that should have taken months, if not years, for her to be able to perform. I've never seen anything like it!"

There was silence for a moment, no doubt while Vargas listened to Robertson, and then he said, "No, I'm not exaggerating. You told me to get in touch and that's what I'm doing. If you don't want her, I'll hand her over to some other agency. You aren't the only one out there, you know!"

More listening.

"Yes, I can hold her here until your man arrives, but I expect to be compensated handsomely for my efforts. It's not easy keeping the "Miracle Woman of Juarez" away from the press. They've been camped out in the lobby since she regained consciousness!"

Another moment of silence, then, "Understood. I'll see to it."

Recognizing that the call was about to end from the finality of Vargas' tone, Gabrielle turned and headed back the way she had come as quickly as she could, not wanting to raise Vargas' suspicions by getting caught near his office.

She'd only taken a few steps, however, when a vision crept up on her and sucker-punched her from behind...

One minute she was hurrying down a darkened hallway and the next all of that fell away with a sickening shift and she found herself standing in the middle of a roadway amidst a desolate landscape.

Blackened, skeletal trees lined the roadside, their limbs

straining outward as if seeking to snatch up any would-be travelers stupid enough to pass this way, while the road was pitted and cracked as if in the aftermath of some terrible bombing. The air was thick with ash and dust, the taste of it on her tongue like that of the grave, forcing her to cover her mouth with her fingers in an effort to keep from breathing the stuff in.

Ahead of her a city burned, no doubt the source of the miasma in the air, its once mighty towers of iron and steel now scorched and twisted, reaching for the heavens like supplicants at the altar as flames wrapped them in their fiery embrace. Behind her, in the distance, a wall of darkness gathered on the horizon and filled the sky above it with storm clouds as black as pitch.

But for all that, the scenery didn't fill her with as much dread as the sense that something was out there on the road behind her, hidden in that darkness.

It was coming in her direction, she realized with a shiver of dread. It wasn't just coming toward her, but it was actively pursuing her, hunting her, and it was getting nearer and nearer with every passing second. She could feel its eyes upon her like fingers crawling slowly up her spine, could feel the need, the hunger, that drove it inexorably in her direction, and she knew that if it caught her things would not go well. The very thought of it finding her caused her legs to shake and her heart to shudder in her chest.

She wanted to run, to get away from there as fast as she could, but when she turned to do just that she discovered that her legs wouldn't move, the fear having short-circuited the commands her brain was sending to her muscles and freezing her in place.

Gabrielle glanced back at seething darkness behind her and was just in time to see it leap forward in a blinkered flash, like something witnessed through the light of a strobe, the storm eating up the distance between them with every stutter of light.

At the rate it was moving, it would be on her in seconds.

Run! her mind screamed at her and this time her legs obeyed as she stumbled forward in what could only charitably be called a controlled fall, nearly coming down on her knees before her feet found their footing beneath her and she turned that stumble into a striding run.

Gabrielle raced forward toward the burning city with no idea of what she was going to do when she reached it but instinctively knowing that hiding in that desolate ruin was better than letting the darkness and whatever horrible thing it contained catch up to her. In the city she had a fighting chance to hide, to survive; out here it would be nothing but a slaughter.

She pushed herself onward, digging deep for every scrap of energy she had but knowing that her pursuer was closing in on her despite her best efforts. Just the sound of the storm alone was enough to tell her that; at first there had been nothing but silence around her, but now she could hear the churning hiss and rumble of the storm and beneath that, the shrieks and howls of her pursuer erupting out of the darkness at the storm's heart.

A quick glance over her shoulder confirmed it for her; the storm, and the thing it contained, had already closed half the distance between them and was no doubt gaining even now. There was no way she was going to make the shelter of the city, not without a miracle, but she wasn't ready to give up just yet. She faced forward, pumping her arms to give her just a bit more momentum.

She barely made another five steps when her foot came down on a loose rock and her ankle twisted out from beneath her. She *felt herself falling and put out her hands to protect her face from the ragged pavement...*

She came back to herself with a gasp, stumbling over her own feet as she fought for equilibrium against her shifting surroundings. The silence of the hallway and the cool tiles beneath her feet told her she was in the hospital, but the lingering sense of pursuit nearly had her running pell-mell down the hallway before she recognized that fact. When she did, she had to lean a hand against the wall and bend over at the waist, sucking air into her lungs in an effort to keep from hyperventilating in reaction to what she'd just been through.

A single thought kept repeating itself in the back of her mind.

What the hell just happened?

Her mind was grappling with the strangeness of it all when the sound of chair legs scraping against the floor reached her ears from inside Vargas' office, reminding her that she might be back in the hospital but she wasn't yet out of danger.

Unwilling to be caught eavesdropping, she forced herself upright and hurried down the hall on silent feet, slipping around the corner just as the door to the office opened and light flooded the hallway behind her.

CHAPTER 12

G ABRIELLE HURRIED BACK TO HER room, intending to change into street clothes and get the heck out of the hospital and out from under Vargas' thumb right that very minute, only to discover a small crimp in her plans.

The wardrobe across from her bed was empty. Her workout sweats had been taken to the laundry. She didn't have any clothes to change into.

For a moment her mind drew a blank as to what to do next and she simply stood there, staring into the wardrobe, until the urgency of her situation asserted herself.

Fine, she thought, glancing down at the hospital gown she was wearing and the thin ties that held it closed. *If I have to walk out of here with my bare ass on display for the world to see, then that's what I'm doing to do. I'm not staying here a second longer!*

Vargas and his mysterious caller had obviously been talking about her and that put her situation in a whole new light. So far she'd been thinking of Vargas and his staff as well-meaning caregivers who were otherwise clueless when it came to the bigger issue that she was dealing with. But what if that wasn't the case? What if Vargas knew exactly what was going on? What if, and here was a paranoid thought but she couldn't just dismiss it, he'd put her into a coma in the first place?

Put Anna into the coma, you mean.

Right.

Anna.

The correction aside, if she was honest with herself, Gabrielle would have to admit that she was already having trouble thinking of herself and Anna as two different people. It had been shocking at first, being in a body different from her own, but over the last several days she'd slowly grown used to seeing a face other than the one she expected when she looked in the mirror. And since she didn't see her old body lying around waiting for her to jump back into it, she was kind of stuck in this one. She had no idea how it had happened but she was here now and that seemed to be that. At least her consciousness and Anna's body seemed to be in synch with each other. If she thought about moving her hands, her hands moved, just as if they'd been her hands since the day that she was born.

But they aren't your hands and you can't forget that.

And therein lay the problem.

If she wasn't careful, she'd go mad.

Maybe I've already started down that road, she thought. There had been several times during the past week where she'd simply lost herself. Not blacked out, as such; at least it didn't feel like that. It was more like stepping away from herself for a time, the way a cell phone suddenly drops the signal only to find it again a few minutes later. Each time she returned, if she could even call it that, she'd be fuzzy-headed and disoriented. It would take several minutes for her thoughts to clear and for her memory to come back.

And let's not forget that little episode you just had back there in the hallway, she told herself.

She didn't know if what she'd seen had been a hallucination or a vision or maybe even one of Anna's leftover memories still lingering about in the cell tissues of her brain. She supposed at this point it really didn't matter. First things first. She'd deal with what she'd seen once she got out of confinement.

It was coming up on 1 am. The nursing staff wouldn't start their rounds for at least another half-an-hour. If she was going to get out of here, now was the time to do it.

Knowing her chances of sneaking out weren't going to improve by waiting, she stepped out of her room and retraced her steps down the hallway, headed for the stairwell just past the exit sign at the far end.

She almost made it.

Gabrielle was less than a yard from the door leading to the stairwell when a voice spoke up from behind her.

"Where are you going?"

For a moment her imagination made it into something it was not, a deep, guttural voice reminiscent of some denizen of the hell. Adrenaline flooded her system at the sound, kicking her heart into overdrive and causing it to beat like a kettledrum in her chest. For just a moment she considered making a break for it, grabbing the door, flinging it open, and charging down the stairs as fast as her feet could carry her, but she knew that doing so would call a lot of attention and that was the last thing she wanted to do. She fought the instinct to run, forced herself to keep it together, and calmly turned around to face her inquisitor.

Who turned out to be nothing more than a young girl.

She couldn't have been older than five or six and stood staring from a nearby room. The girl had curly, blonde hair that came down to her shoulders and was dressed in a long, white nightgown with the Little Mermaid on the front of it. She looked up at Gabrielle and repeated her question.

"Where are you going?"

This time Gabrielle heard it for what it was, the voice of a child, full of innocent questions.

"For a little walk," she replied, smiling.

The girl took that in and then looked up and down the hallway, taking in the darkened corridor on either side. Gabrielle had the distinct sense that the child was making sure they weren't being overheard. When it was clear that they weren't, the girl turned back to face her and in an exaggerated whisper said, "But you're in your PJs like me!"

Gabrielle's relief was so great that she wanted to laugh, but she stifled it, not wanting to offend the youngster. She bent a bit lower, bringing her closer to the girl's level.

"And I forgot my shoes, too," she said with a grin, lifting one foot off the floor and wiggling her toes, making the girl laugh. "But I won't tell if you won't."

"Do I look like a tattletale?" the girl asked.

"Not at all."

"That's cuz I'm not one."

And thank God for that, Gabrielle thought. To the girl she said, "I've got to get going. See you later!"

"Not if I see you first!" the girl said with a giggle and then slipped back inside the room.

No sooner had the girl turned away than Gabrielle pushed open the door to the stairwell and headed downward at a rapid pace, knowing that every minute that passed was another minute in which her absence could be noticed.

She raced down the last set of stairs and reached for the door leading to the lobby only to stop herself at the last moment when the swell of noise from the other side of the door caught her attention.

It was the dead of night and still the faithful remained, waiting for their chance to meet "Santa Anna."

Gabrielle knew immediately that she couldn't open that door. Going back up the stairs was out of the question; they'd find her missing from her room soon enough and when that happened she wanted as few floors between her and the outside world as possible. Which meant she had only one other choice available.

Down.

The stairwell in which she stood went down one more floor. Perhaps she could find an emergency exit or a way to access the parking garage from down there somewhere, allowing her to get out of the building. Frankly anything was better than having to fight her way through the crowd in the lobby.

Turning, she headed down the stairs.

CHAPTER 13

REACHING THE BOTTOM OF THE steps, Gabrielle emerged into a long corridor running perpendicular to the stairs. Unlike the brightly illuminated hallways of the floors above, this one was deserted, the lab techs and staff workers having long since gone home for the evening. It was lit only by an occasional overhead light along its length, allowing pools of shadow to gather and lurk in the spaces between. Despite the dim light, she could see that there were doors set at regular intervals on either side and a red sign flickered off and on all the way down at the far end to her left.

Salida, it read.

Exit.

Gabrielle headed for it with a quickened step.

She passed darkened rooms with names she didn't recognize etched on the door glass, but ignored them, intent on reaching the sign and the exit it signified. Normally she didn't mind the dark, but something about this place – perhaps the late hour or the things she'd overhead on the phone earlier – had her feeling spooked. The sooner she reached the exit and got out, the better.

She had just reached the end of the hall when she heard the elevator ding behind her.   She ignored it, turning the corner...only to stop short.

Another hall stretched before her, nearly identical to the one she had just left, except this one ended in an emergency exit. The door was propped open and an orderly leaned against it, standing in the circle of light just beyond smoking a cigarette.

The orderly's attention was fully focused on enjoying his smoke and he didn't appear to have noticed her, standing there in the shadows.   Perhaps the exterior light kept him from seeing much in this direction, she didn't know. She was just glad he hadn't looked in her direction when she'd come around the corner.   Moving as slowly and as quietly as she could, she backed up a step and peeked around the corner.

A second orderly, head down and hands in his pockets, was headed her way, having just stepped off the elevator and most likely headed for a rendezvous with his buddy outside.

If they saw her, she was finished.

Dressed as she was, it was clear she was a patient; they'd return her to her room where the nurse would most likely give her something to help her sleep and keep her from wandering off.

She couldn't allow that to happen.

For a moment she considered trying to bluff her way past the orderly at the door, but an inner voice told her that wasn't the way.   Instead, she pulled her head back around the corner, and moving as quietly as she could she stepped to the nearest door and tried the knob.

Locked.

She looked down the hall, noted that the orderly hadn't moved from his position outside, and slipped over to the next door down the hall, only to find that it, too, was locked up tight.

Now she could hear footsteps approaching behind her as the second orderly drew closer.

Another glance ahead with still no change in the first orderly's position convinced her to move closer and try again.

Come on, come on, she thought, as she grabbed the door knob.

At first she thought that this one was locked too, but when she used a little more force she distinctly heard the latch click beneath her hands and felt the door swing open into the darkened room beyond.

Gabrielle didn't hesitate, just threw herself inside and closed the door as quickly and as quietly as she could manage. Not knowing where she was or what she might stumble over if she tried to move around the room in the dark, she crouched down with her back pressed against the door, praying that she hadn't been seen.

Outside in the hall, she heard footsteps approaching and she froze, not daring to move, not even to breathe.

The steps drew closer...

Closer...

...and then began to recede as the orderly passed the door she was hiding behind, calling out in Spanish to his friend down the hall.

Gabrielle let out the breath she'd been holding in a rush of relief.

So far, so good, she thought.

She was trapped in a room in the hospital basement with two orderlies less than fifty feet away, but that was still a damn sight better than remaining in her room waiting for whatever it was that Dr. Vargas had planned for her.

All she had to do was wait for the orderlies to finish their smoke break and skip out the exit at the end of the hall with no one the wiser.

She could hear the orderlies talking and joking with each other, so she knew they were still there. As the minutes ticked past with nothing more to do but wait, Gabrielle began to get curious about the room she was standing in. Perhaps there was something here that she could use once she escaped from the hospital. It seemed like it was worth a look.

She didn't dare turn on the light as she was afraid it would easily be seen shining into the corridor from underneath the door. Instead she stood up, keeping her back to the door, and reached out with her hands, first on her right, where she found a counter of some sort, and then on her left, where her hands discovered some clothing hanging on a rack.

Lab coats.

She carefully took one down from the rack, doing everything she could not to make any noise while doing so, then squatted down and laid the coat lengthwise against the crack beneath the door, forcing it into the gap with her fingertips. Satisfied, she stood up, felt along the wall for a light switch and, finding it, flicked it on.

Brilliant white fluorescent light flooded the room, causing her to blink several times against the brightness. A quick glance toward her feet told her that she didn't have to worry about the light leaking out into the corridor; the lab coat completely filled the gap beneath the door and then some.

Satisfied, Gabrielle looked around the room, discovering as she did so that she was standing in the hospital morgue.

Lovely.

The room was much larger than she expected, stretching out

lengthwise in front of her, with three autopsy tables laid out in the center, the first and third of which held bodies draped in white linen, and several large metal sinks along the right wall. Opposite those, on the other side of the room, were cold storage drawers in three sets of four. Seeing them, Gabrielle found herself wondering just how many of them were occupied. A computer workstation, currently shut down, a counter containing various scales, specimen containers, and a stack of files, with a whiteboard hanging on the wall behind it, filled the rest of the space. Beneath the counter were several long drawers.

She hurried over and began quietly opening one drawer after another, until she hit the jackpot; this drawer was filled with folded sets of light blue hospital scrubs. She found some that looked like they would fit her, then stripped off her hospital gown and pulled them on. They were a little large, especially the pants, but the drawstring allowed her to cinch them up tight enough to make do.

Now if I can only find some shoes...

She nervously went through the rest of the drawers, conscious that someone could walk in at any moment, but in the end she was glad that she did for she found a set of tennis shoes, tagged as evidence and most likely from one of the deceased on the tables behind her, that, while too large to be comfortable, would do well enough for the time being.

Her spirits now buoyed significantly by the simple fact that she was dressed enough to at least appear in public. She turned and surveyed the room again. From where she stood, Gabrielle could now see two other exits from the room. The first was to her left, next to the cold-storage drawers, and had a sign hanging over it that read Family Viewing. The second, directly opposite her on the far side of the room past the autopsy tables, also had a sign. This one read Ambulance Bay.

Gabrielle's heart leapt at the sight and she hurried across the room toward it.

She was halfway across the room, just passing the center autopsy table, when the lights went out and the sudden scent of ozone, like right after a lightning strike, filled the air.

What the hell?

Gabrielle came to an immediate halt, afraid of banging something and giving herself away to the men out in the hall. The smell was there for a moment and gone again, just as quickly as it had come. She brushed it aside as a hefty whiff of leftover cleaning agent and focused instead on dealing with the darkness in which she found herself. She put her hands out, feeling around, until her fingers found the edge of the autopsy table. She grabbed it and pulled herself over to it, but was careful not to feel around any further; she didn't want to put her hands on the body she knew was lying just inches away.

Gabrielle was tough; she'd been through literal hell since the Adversary had seized her in its grip on that summer night so many years ago. She'd seen more than her fair share of horrors and had survived them all, including having her body possessed by an evil so ancient it made the mountains seem young. She knew how to handle herself in a tough situation. But there was something about being trapped in a darkened room with only the dead for company that sent a primal shiver of fear down her spine. She knew there wasn't anything here that could hurt her – the orderlies in the hall were a far bigger threat to her freedom – but the sooner she got out of here, the better.

As she stood there in the darkness, she thought she heard someone whisper her name.

Not her assumed name, but her real one.

Gabrielle.

She turned slowly in place, her ears straining to pick up the sound again even as she told herself she had to be imagining it. No one here knew her by that name; it had to be her mind playing tricks on her.

When the lights came back on she glanced about, startled and needing to confirm that she was still, indeed, alone.

Not alone, an inner voice said. *You have the dead for company.*

"But the dead don't speak," she answered aloud, feeling foolish but for some reason needing the reassurance of hearing her voice, "or turn off the lights."

The whispering she could put down to her imagination, but the lights?

Faulty wiring, she told herself. *That's all it was.*

Before she could convince herself otherwise she started toward the ambulance bay door again but had only taken a few steps when she heard the rustle of a sheet behind her, followed almost immediately by that whisper again.

"Gabrielle..."

She whirled about.

The corpse that had been lying flat on the autopsy table behind her just seconds before was now sitting straight up as if held erect by unseen marionette strings, the sheet still draped over it like a ghost.

This isn't happening, she thought distantly, as the flesh on her arms broke out in goose bumps and her hair tried to stand on end.

The sound was coming from the corpse; she was certain of it.

Run! an inner voice commanded, but she didn't listen to it, strangely captivated by the sight of the corpse sitting there whispering her name.

She took a step toward it, her arm coming up as if intending to pull off the sheet, to see if the corpse was really whispering to her or if this was all in her head.

As if on cue, the six cold-storage drawers to her right rolled open with a clatter, drawing her attention. She looked on, stunned, as the corpses there jerked upright, their covered faces turning as one to "stare" in her direction.

The room began to fill with the sound of the newly dead whispering her name.

She broke then, turning away from the drawers and their suddenly talkative occupants, intent to get the hell out of there as fast as her feet would carry her, only to find the corpse that had been lying on the last autopsy table now blocking her access to the ambulance bay.

He'd been a big man in life and death seemed to have only made him more solid-looking. He was naked, the grayish-purple color of his flesh broken by the thick lines of the surgical stitches running in a Y-shape from just above his crotch up and across his chest to toward either shoulder. His eyes, white with death cataracts, focused on her.

The corpse tried to smile, its facial muscles twitching, but was prevented from doing so by the thread holding its lips together. Thwarted, it decided on a different course of action, shooting its arms out unexpectedly and locking its thick fingers around Gabrielle's throat.

Then it began to squeeze.

For a second her brain stuttered like a record caught in a groove, her rational mind trying to make sense of the craziness going on around her, and then her instinct for survival asserted itself.

Gabrielle exploded into action without conscious thought, her body seeming to remember what to do in a situation like this faster than her brain had even started to comprehend. Rather than wasting time trying to pry the finger away from her throat, which is what most people who've found themselves in such a situation would do, Gabrielle brought her arms up sharply, striking the underside of the corpse's arms with her own just in front of its elbows. The explosive movement tore its hands free of her, letting precious air flood her already bruising throat.

She wasn't finished there, however. Already inside the corpse's reach, she turned partially sideways and delivered a vicious kick to the corpse's right knee, shattering the joint and compromising its ability to stand upright. As it started to tumble forward, she continued her turn, lashing out with her elbow to strike the corpse in the side of the head. The blow was strong enough to twist the corpse's head three-quarters of the way around and Gabrielle heard the audible snap of vertebrae.

That should have been enough – would have been enough if she'd been fighting a human opponent; the strike was powerful enough to incapacitate, if not kill outright. But this was not a living, breathing person and the force animating it did not care about the physical condition of that body it occupied.

Head hanging at an odd angle and one leg dragging behind it, the corpse reached for her again.

Gabrielle kicked out again, striking the corpse square in the face and sending it over backward.

Behind her, the rustling of sheets let her know the other corpses were headed in her direction.

Time to get the hell out!

Not wanting to risk leaping over the still-twitching corpse,

Gabrielle vaulted over the now-empty autopsy table and ran for the door. She hit it on the run, no longer caring about making noise, and sent it crashing against the wall as she raced through the doorway.

She found herself standing outside the hospital, the streets of Jaurez stretching out before her.

Without glancing back, she headed off into the night.

CHAPTER 14

GABRIELLE RAN DOWN SEVERAL STREETS, not caring so much where she was going as simply wanting to put as much distance between herself and the hospital as she could. She had no idea if they would come after her, but if they did, she didn't want to make it easy for them.

It was only when she finally stopped to catch her breath in the shadow of a building some distance from the hospital that the reality of her situation finally caught up with her. Animating corpses aside, she was in a foreign country with no money, no identification, and no idea how she was going to get across the border, never mind travel halfway across the country in order to find her husband, Cade. All she had were the scrubs on her back and a pair of stolen shoes on her feet, plus the information she was carrying in her head about what the Adversary had done. While the later was potentially earth-shattering news, it wouldn't buy her a ham sandwich, never mind get her across the border.

Juarez wasn't exactly the safest place in Mexico, she knew. She'd been in the city long enough to understand that it was a hotbed of violence, with multiple drug cartels battling it out across the city streets. The number of people dying on the streets of Juarez was second only to the number of people who vanished without a trace, casualties of the same war.

Americans could be targets here, she knew, particularly to protest the continuing aid being sent to Mexico by the American government, aid that helped fuel the drug war. For the first time since waking up in Anna Rodriquez's body, Gabriel was thankful for her decidedly Hispanic appearance. It would let her move through the city streets without being immediately picked out as a foreigner. Her newfound affinity for the Spanish language would no doubt help as well.

Now she just needed a plan.

For a moment she toyed with the idea of presenting herself to the Border patrol at the checkpoint and identifying herself as a U.S. citizen in trouble, hoping they'd at least listen to her story, but that would no doubt bring her situation to the attention of the US military once they scanned her prints into the system. The Marine Corps might have honorably discharged her after her accident, but that didn't mean they wouldn't want to talk to her again when they found out she'd not only miraculously recovered from her coma but walked out of the hospital under her own power just a few weeks later. She could see herself disappearing down some government rabbit hole for further testing and never being heard from again. Thanks but no thanks to that one.

Same went for the U.S. embassy.

Without the help of either of those agencies, she didn't see a way of getting across the border legally, which meant she was going to have to choose a less respectable means of entering the country.

Like crossing illegally on foot.

She glanced around, trying to get her bearings, but the only parts of Juarez she'd seen had been from the window of her hospital room and down here at street level everything looked the same.

Gabrielle looked up instead, searching the night sky until she found the North Star. Regardless of where she was in Juarez, it was a simple fact of geometry that the United States was north of her position. By following the star, she would at least be heading in the right direction.

She began making her way through the winding streets, heading north where and whenever possible. It was late and there were only a few people out on the streets at this hour. Gabrielle avoided them, hiding in the shadows until they passed by or taking an alternate route around them if she spotted them in time to do so. She kept to the side streets, not liking the lights or the vehicular traffic on the main thoroughfares, slipping from one to the next like a ghost in the night.

Occasionally a car would come in her direction. Each time she would quickly find a doorway or an alley to hide in and wait for it to pass, worried not just about being a woman alone at night in a deserted, and if appearances were any indication, dangerous area, but also about pursuit. She hoped Vargas would just let her go once he discovered that she was missing, but something told her it wouldn't be that easy. She didn't want to take the chance of flagging down an approaching vehicle only to discover it was someone he'd sent out after her from the hospital staff with orders to bring her in.

Eventually she found herself in a more commercial district, with signs leading to Highway 45, and her eyes lit up at the sight. Once it crossed the border, Highway 45 became US Route 54, leading into the heart of El Paso.

Getting there, she thought.

Another half hour of walking brought her to the access road, but it was what stood on the other side of it that caught her attention.

A truck stop.

The lights drew her like a moth to a flame.

CHAPTER 15

THE TRUCK STOP WAS ONE of those chains that served the long hauler routes running across the southwestern United States and into Mexico. It was part convenience store, part restaurant, and part locker room, with showers, toilets, and hot food available twenty-four-seven. A wide selection of items were available for purchase in the store, everything from ready-made sandwiches and snacks to motor oil and antifreeze.

The place was brilliantly lit even at this late hour thanks to a dozen overhead fluorescent lamps hanging from the ceiling and the light made her feel exposed as she came in the door, like everyone in the place was watching her.

In truth, only a few of the customers even glanced in her direction and those that did quickly dismissed her as insignificant and went back to what they were doing.

Gabrielle walked deeper into the store, doing what she could to get out of the view of the clerk behind the counter. She didn't want anyone to put two and two together from the news reports being broadcast from the hospital lobby and possibly recognize her.

She wandered over to a rack of long-sleeved shirts and began looking through them, knowing she was going to need something more substantial than the surgical scrubs she was wearing if she hoped to remain inconspicuous while traveling. She found a dark-colored shirt that looked like it would help keep her warm and held it up, measuring it against her body, while at the same time looking around to see if anyone was paying attention.

She was thinking about stealing the shirt, just stuffing it inside the waistband of her scrubs and walking out the front door with no one the wiser since she didn't have any money with her, when a voice spoke up quietly from her right.

"I wouldn't do that if I were you."

She turned to find a heavyset man dressed in a cowboy hat, jeans, and a pale blue chambrois shirt looking through the rack of clothes next to her. He must have just stepped up, for she hadn't seen him when she'd looked around. He didn't even so much as glance at her, but she knew it had to have been him that had spoken. She also noticed his decidedly American accent.

"Excuse me?" she said.

He kept looking through the rack of clothing, speaking again in the same soft tones. "There's a camera over your shoulder and a large Mexican at the front door with orders to stop any would-be shoplifters. So I'd forget about stashin' that shirt, if I was you."

Gabrielle felt a chill run up her spine. *Who was this guy? How had he known what she was going to do? Had the authorities caught up with her already?*

She glanced around nervously, but didn't see anyone else paying the two of them any attention. She might still be able to get out of here if...

He turned to face her for the first time, his hands held out in a non-threatening way.

"Look, relax, okay? I'm not going to turn you in or nothin'. You look like a woman in trouble," – this last bit said with a sad smile – "and I wouldn't be the man I like to think I am if I didn't offer you some help."

"I didn't ask for your help," Gabrielle said quickly.

"No, you didn't, that's true. But I'm going to offer it anyway. Cuz you look like you could use it. How about you let me buy you a cup of coffee or something in the café over there and you can decide what you want to do after that, alright? At least then I'll have done something and my conscience will give me a break."

She looked over at the cafeteria-like coffee shop he was referring to, where a tired-looking waitress was waiting on a handful of customers who didn't look all that different from the man next to her. All long-haul truckers, it seemed, on their way out or headed back home.

Home...

Just like that she realized she might have found a way of getting across the border. If she played her cards right.

The café, if you could call it that, was well-lit and there were plenty of others around if this guy turned out to be something other than what he purported to be. Besides, she hadn't eaten in hours.

Gabrielle let go of the t-shirt she'd been fingering and found herself nodding in agreement. "All right," she said, with a shy smile, "a cup of coffee sounds good."

# # #

The man's name turned out to be Stan - Stan Greenville - and he was exactly what Gabrielle had hoped; a long-haul trucker headed back to the States with a fresh load of produce in the back of his semi-trailer. He and Gabrielle were seated in a corner booth in the back of the coffee shop where there was little chance of them being overheard by the other patrons, few though there were. They'd ordered breakfast and he'd waited until she was three-quarters of the way finished before speaking up.

"Boyfriend or husband?"

Gabrielle looked up at him in confusion. "I'm sorry?"

"You have some significant bruises around your neck, the kind you don't get by accident," Stan said gently. "You're wearing scrubs, which suggest that you've recently been hospitalized. You don't appear to have any money, otherwise you've wouldn't have tried to steal that shirt, and you're obviously running from someone or something. That suggests an abusive man in your life. So, boyfriend or husband?"

"Boyfriend," Gabrielle said, picking up the thread he was laying down before her and running with it, hoping it might be her ticket to getting out of here before Vargas, the FBI, or whatever that thing back at the hospital had been, caught up with her.

"And?"

Gabrielle spun a yarn about crossing the border with her boyfriend on a lark, just a stupid night out on the town in Mexico, until he'd gotten drunk and accused her of flirting with another man. Last thing she remembered was him beating and choking her into unconsciousness. She'd woken up in the hospital the next day without any money or identification to prove who she was and deathly afraid that her boyfriend might find her and finish the job he'd started the night before.

"So I snuck out the first chance I got," she said, "and here I am."

Stan nodded, as if that was exactly what he expected to hear. "You got family, someone you can call to help you out?"

She shook her head. "No. Mom died years ago and I never knew my father."

Stan watched her put down a few more bites of her meal without saying anything. Gabrielle could tell that he was on the verge of making some kind of decision, so she kept her mouth shut, waiting to see what would happen, not wanting to say the wrong thing and blow it.

"Look," Stan began, "You're clearly in trouble and I'd like to help you out. Really I would. But how do I know you aren't just feeding me a line of bullshit? That you're not one of them, you know, illegals, trying to sneak into the country and using me to do it?"

For a moment, Gabrielle couldn't believe he was serious. Given everything she had been through, his concern seemed so trivial that it took all her effort not to laugh in his face. Here she was, in someone else's body running from animated corpses and corrupt doctor's who wanted to sell her to the FBI for heaven's sake, and her Good Samaritan was worried she might be an illegal immigrant!

If she laughed, though, she knew she'd lose him for sure, so she quashed the desire to do so, her thoughts whirling as she tried to come up with an answer that would satisfy him. Her gaze drifted over him, taking in the worn by serviceable work-shirt with the sleeves rolled up to mid-forearm, the hint of an old tattoo that peaked out from beneath the cuff...

That was it!

Gabrielle reached up and pulled the collar of her scrubs away from her neck, revealing the tattoo of the eagle, globe and anchor that snaked up the side of her neck from her shoulder.

"I don't know too many illegals who have one of these, do you?"

Stan leaned forward and examined the tattoo for a moment. "What was your unit?" he asked.

Gabrielle had absolutely no idea but the answer popped out of her mouth anyway. "Two tours in Iraq with Lima Company, 3rd Battalion, 8th Marines."

Where the hell had that come from? she wondered.

Stan nodded, but apparently wasn't yet convinced. "So you saw some heavy action in Rawah, huh?"

"No," she replied, shaking her head. "Fallujah and Ramadi, but not Rawah."

Truth was Gabrielle wouldn't have been able to tell one from the other, hell, she couldn't even locate either of them on a map, but she must have said something right for Stan suddenly relaxed, leaning back in his seat with a smile on his face.

He pushed the rolled-up cuff of his right sleeve higher, revealing a similar, though much more faded, tattoo on his own arm. He caught and held her gaze.

"Semper Fi," he said, with a solemn nod.

Gabrielle nodded back.

"Semper Fi."

CHAPTER 16

ONCE A MARINE, ALWAYS A Marine, or so the saying goes, and Stan took that saying very seriously indeed, it seemed. The minute he was convinced that Gabrielle was who she said she was – a fellow Marine stranded far from home – there was no further question about whether or not he would help her, just a focus on how to get it done.

Stan had seen door-to-door fighting in the city of Hue in a little country called Vietnam, oh so many years ago, and he'd never forgotten the experience. He'd been assigned to the 2nd Battalion, 5th Marines, he told her, and while their experiences were several decades apart, he knew exactly what she'd been through.

He promised he'd see her across the border and on her way home. After all, Marines never left one of their own behind.

"Come on," he said. "I think I've got some clothes that might fit you out in the truck."

He paid the check, then led her out of the café and across the parking lot to where his rig was parked. He was driving a red

Peterbilt sleeper cab and trailer that had clearly been lovingly maintained over the years despite seeing its fair share of long hard hauls. A World War II style pin-up logo showing a big-busted woman in a short skirt sitting atop a bomb with a burning fuse decorated the door, with the words "Mighty Bertha" painted underneath in bright yellow letters.

"This here's my girl," Stan said proudly, patting the side of the cab with obvious affection. "We've seen and done a lot of things together over the years; nowadays, I don't go anywhere without her."

He unlocked the cab and climbed inside, disappearing into the back for a few minutes before returning with some clothes in hand.

"My nephew ran a couple of hauls with me last fall and left these behind," he told her. "Lucky for you, I never got around to sending them back."

He handed her a pair of jeans, a couple of dark-colored t-shirts, and a long-sleeved flannel over-shirt. Pointing to the cab, he said, "Climb up inside Bertha there and see if they fit."

Anything was better than the thin medical scrubs she was wearing, so she did as he suggested. The sleeper section of the cab was roomier than she imagined, with a full-size bed, a small closet, and a shelving unit with a built-in wide screen television. Drapes covered the windows, ensuring privacy for the driver when resting for the night.

Gabrielle stripped off her scrubs and pulled on the clothing she'd been given. The pants were a bit too long, but nothing that couldn't be cured by rolling the cuffs a time or two. The t-shirt fit fairly well, as did the flannel over-shirt, and Gabrielle felt her spirits rise thanks to the fresh clothing and her new ally. After a long hard night, things were finally looking up.

Stan gave her a once-over when she climbed back out of the truck and then nodded with approval. "Yep, that'll do."

"Now what?" Gabrielle asked.

"Now we get you across the border. Climb on up there," he said, pointing at the passenger seat, "and I'll explain on the way."

Despite its age, the truck was quieter and more comfortable than she expected. Gabrielle watched as Stan deftly maneuvered the big vehicle out of the truck stop parking lot and drove up the ramp onto Highway 54.

"I've been driving this route for almost a decade now and know most of the guys working the border entry. Nine times out of ten they check my paperwork and wave me through without a second glance.

"So when the time comes, you're going to climb into the back of the cab and I'm going to shut these drapes right here," he said, pointing to the heavy curtains hanging to the right of the passenger seat she was sitting in, "and roll on through with them none the wiser."

Gabrielle frowned. "Won't having the curtain closed look suspicious when we get to the checkpoint? What if they want to search the cab?"

"They won't."

Stan seemed pretty convinced that they'd be okay, but Gabrielle wasn't so certain. The whole idea sounded a bit preposterous, in fact. If it was that easy, illegal immigrants would be crossing the border by the car load rather than hiding out in specially built vehicles or paying coyotes to sneak them across the border on foot.

Stan must have seen the conflict playing out on her face for he reached out and gently touched her arm. "It will be okay. I promised I'd get you across and I will. Trust me. Please."

Trust is in short supply these days, Gabrielle thought, but she really didn't have much choice in the matter. Unless she wanted to swim the Rio Grande and hike across Texas on her own, Stan was the best chance she had of getting back to the States.

"All right then," she said, leaning back in her chair, "let's do this."

#   #   #

It took them half an hour to reach the bridge leading to the United States.

"'Bout time you made yourself scarce," Stan said, as they pulled onto the bridge and began the slow crawl through traffic toward the border crossing on the far side.

Gabrielle patted him on the arm for luck and then slipped between the two seats into the sleeper portion of the cab, pulling the thick curtain shut behind her and using the clips along one edge to seal it closed.

Here we go, she thought.

The truck rumbled forward for another five minutes or so before the loud hiss of the air brakes reached her ears as Stan brought the big rig to a halt.

Gabrielle heard the window go down and then the ring of someone's boots outside.

"Morning," Stan said, to whoever it was.

"Papers, please."

There was a moment of silence, no doubt while the border guard examined Stan's passport. Gabrielle sat on the edge of the bed, not daring to move and doing her best to breathe as quietly as possible.

"What's in the rig, Mr. Greenville?"

"Diesel fuel pumps. I've got a full load bound for Chicago."

"Would you mind opening it up, please?"

Gabrielle's heart skipped a beat.

Relax, she told herself. *Examining the cargo is probably standard procedure.*

But Stan's next words told her it wasn't standard at all.

"Is there something wrong with the paperwork?" he asked.

The guard ignored his question. "Please open the back of your rig, Mr. Greenville," he said.

There was no mistaking the man's "I'm being patient but don't fuck with me" tone.

Stan apparently heard the warning loud and clear.

"All right, all right. Hold your horses," he said. "I'm a comin'."

Gabrielle heard the door open and the cab rise slightly as Stan stepped down to the road. A few moments passed and then the squeal of a heavy door in need of lubricant reached her ears from the back of the trailer. She sat on the bunk in the sleeper cab, tense, straining her ears to hear what was being said back there but there was too much metal and distance between them for her to make out anything clearly.

The door clanged shut.

For a moment Gabrielle thought it might be over.

Then she heard the guard and Stan talking again right outside the cab.

"I'll need to see inside the sleeper unit as well."

Inside the sleeper unit? Shit!

Gabrielle glanced around frantically, looking for somewhere that she could hide in the now-seemingly tiny compartment. She knew she had only seconds before that door opened and she couldn't be here, in plain view, when it did.

Unfortunately, there was nowhere for her to go.

The space beneath the bed was occupied by a set of built-in drawers. The mini-closet was just that – mini. It was located above the far end of the bed and barely had enough room to hold the handful of shirts and coats currently hanging inside it, never mind the fact that it didn't have a door she could pull shut behind her. If she slipped through the curtain to the other side, she'd no doubt be visible to anyone standing outside the vehicle.

She could crawl beneath the bed sheets she was sitting on, but the border agent would have to be blind not to see her lying there.

She was trapped!

Panic brought her to her feet, but it was too late. Even as she turned about, seeking a solution that simply wasn't there, the door to her left opened and the immigration officer stuck his head inside the sleeper cab less than three feet from where she stood.

He was young, in his mid-thirties was Gabrielle's first guess, and dressed in the dark green uniform of the U.S. Border Patrol. Her gaze traveled from his face, down to the pistol holstered at his side, and back up again. His gaze locked with hers and Gabrielle waited for him to sound the alarm as the moment stretched for what felt like hours.

Then, without a word or even a visual acknowledgment that he had seen her, the officer stepped back down and shut the door, leaving Gabrielle staring at its blank surface.

"Paperwork is in order; you're good to go."

Gabrielle stood there, shaking, stunned at what had just happened.

Good to go?

"Thank you, officer," Stan said, as he climbed back up into the cab and slammed the door behind him. "Have a good day."

The engine rumbled into life and Gabrielle had to grab for the bed behind her to keep from falling to the floor as Stan put the rig into drive and pulled back onto the road.

Gabrielle sat there in disbelief, shaking from the adrenaline that had dumped into her system, until Stan said, "We're clear. You can come out now."

She opened the curtain and climbed into the passenger seat just as the "Welcome to the United States" sign flashed by along the side of the road. She'd never been happier to see five little words.

"How on earth…?"

Stan grinned and waved his fingers in her direction. "These are not the droids you are looking for."

Gabrielle had no idea what he was talking about. Her blank stare must have informed him of such, for after a moment he gave an embarrassed chuckle and said, "Sorry. Just ignore me; sometimes I'm too much of a geek for my own good."

"Okaaaay, but that still doesn't tell me how we got past that immigration officer."

Stan shrugged. "Would you believe blind luck?"

"No."

He nodded thoughtfully for a moment and then said, "I've been running this route for a lot of years now. From time to time I try and help out those in need. When I do, my friends in the Border Patrol look the other way."

Gabrielle stared at him skeptically. "What? Purely out of the kindness of their hearts?"

"Well, that and a few crisp five hundred dollar bills in their pockets."

Now things were making a bit more sense.

No wonder he was so convinced they wouldn't have a problem, she thought. *He already had that squared away.*

"So, where's the money come from?" she wanted to know.

"Most of it comes out of my own pocket, but sometimes like-minded folks chip in with a donation here and there to keep things running smoothly."

"Strangers give up their hard-earned money just to help those who can't help themselves?"

He nodded. "Yep. That about sums it up."

To Gabrielle's surprise, she believed him. The fact that he didn't try to justify any of it, that he didn't offer some long-winded explanation designed to win her over to his point of view worked in his favor and gave his words an undercurrent of authenticity that would have been lost otherwise. In the end, she came to the conclusion that Stan was exactly what he claimed to be; an honest man going out of his way to help others in need.

Just as he was doing.

"Well, then, you have my thanks."

He glanced over at her and smiled for a second before turning his attention back to the road. "You're quite welcome," he said.

They were quiet for a time, just letting the tires eat up the road as they headed north through Texas, each lost in their own thoughts. Eventually, Stan turned to her and said, "I'm headed north, up through Texas, Arkansas, and Missouri, then on into Illinois. You're welcome to ride with me as far as you'd like or I can drop you off anywhere along the way."

Gabrielle nodded. "I appreciate that," she said. "I'll let you know once I've figured out what I'm going to do."

"Take your time; no rush. We've got a lot of miles to cover

before we get to the end of this journey."

Truer words have never been spoken.

Gabrielle leaned back against the seat and, staring out the window at the lightening sky, considered her options.

Her first order of business was getting in touch with her husband, Cade. She knew that much, at least. But just how she was going to manage it? Well, that was another thing entirely.

For one, she had no idea where Cade was or what he was doing. Heck, she didn't even know if he was still alive, for heaven's sake!

No, wait, she thought. Scratch that. She did know; Cade WAS alive. Of that she was certain. It didn't matter how full of holes her memory might be; if Cade were dead, she'd know it all the way down to the depths of her soul. She loved him too deeply for it to be any other way. He was out there, somewhere. She was sure of it.

So where was he?

That was the question, wasn't it?

That vague notion that she should be traveling northeast was still with her and she concentrated on that for awhile, wondering where it was coming from and what it meant. The more she tried to force it, the faster understanding seemed to recede. Frustrated, she blew out a breath and let it go, focusing instead on the memories of her husband. She called his face to mind, remembering how quick he'd been to laugh and the way he would reach up to push his long hair off his face even after he'd cut it away to meet uniform regulations...

Gabrielle's eyes popped open in surprise as the memory of the way her husband had looked in his dark uniform surged to the surface.

Cade had been a...firefighter?

No, a cop, she realized.

And not just any cop, but a member of the Special Tactics and Operations Team, a real type-A go-getter when it came to fighting crime and going after the bad guys. She remembered joking with him once, telling him he would have been that lone Sheriff facing off against a gang of gunfighters all on his own if he'd lived in the Old West and he'd laughed, asking where he'd left his white horse.

She felt her pulse quickening at the memory. Mentally calling up a map of the eastern seaboard, she ran her finger up the coast, hoping the names might jar something else loose.

Baltimore?

Philadelphia?

Newark?

New York?

None of them felt quite right.

Then memory stirred once more and her mental finger moved further east along the map, sliding up through Connecticut, Rhode Island and into Massachusetts until it landed on the city of Boston.

The image of her husband standing tall in his uniform rose within her thoughts and she remembered rubbing her fingers across the brass just above his pocket as she leaned in for a kiss before he left on patrol...

BPD.

Boston Police Department.

That was it!

She grinned like the Cheshire Cat, her satisfaction at having actually remembered something important only slightly tempered by the fact that Boston was a long way off.

So be it, she thought. Better a far destination than no

destination at all.

Gabrielle glanced at Stan's cell phone, sitting upright in the cup holder between them. She thought about using it, just picking it up and placing a call to the department switchboard, asking to be connected to Officer Williams, but she didn't need to be thinking clearly to understand that was a bad idea. What was she going to say? Hi Cade, it's your wife, Gabrielle. Long time no talk, yeah? She didn't think so. Primarily because she knew it was true; it had been a long time since the two of them had spoken. Her memory was spotty as hell, but she knew that much. Just calling him out of the blue was going to make him think someone was trying to mess with his head and that certainly wouldn't end well.

If by some miracle he didn't think her call was some kind of cruel prank and hang up in her face, she would have an even bigger hurdle to face in explaining where she had been all this time.

Especially since she didn't know herself.

No, she thought, *best to get to Boston and decide out what to do from there.* Finding Cade was the first step. She'd figure out how to approach him once she'd tracked him down.

Decision made, Gabrielle turned back to staring out the window at the scenery flowing past. Eventually, the monotony of the landscape and the rumble of the big rig's engine lulled her to sleep.

The visions came almost as soon as she closed her eyes.

A man in tattered clothing stood on a rocky crag, sword in hand. A pack of horrid creatures surrounded him, their multi-legged bodies moving with sinuous grace as they tried to pull him from his perch, but the man was holding his own for now, slashing and stabbing with his sword to keep them at bay. As the man moved about, Gabrielle caught a look at his face, including the long scar that bisected one half of it, stretching from just above his ruined eye to down along his jawline...

Men in dark fatigues carrying submachine guns race through the growing dark, with those in the rear occasionally stopping to fire back in the direction they had come. Gabrielle can't see anything there beyond the growing darkness that was covering the land in their wake, but she knew from the expressions on their faces that they were frightened of whatever it was that was back there, but, like soldiers the world over, they were doing what needed to be done regardless of that fear...

A delegation of four men and one woman, all dressed to the nines, enter an audience chamber through a set of oversized double doors. A loud voice announces their arrival in a language Gabrielle doesn't understand nor recognize. The delegates ignore it, their attention focused on the figure seated atop a dais at the far end of the audience chamber. As they draw closer, Gabrielle is able to make out more of the details and what she sees makes her breath catch in her throat. The throne the individual is sitting on appears to be made entirely of skulls, human skulls no less, their empty eye sockets staring in accusation at the approaching delegation. The figure seated on the throne of skulls is equally disturbing; tall and gaunt, with eyes of solid black set within a face of dusty grey, his teeth filed to fine points. The men in the delegation stop at the foot of the dais, but the woman continues until she stands directly in front of the throne. The room around them is utterly silent as the seated figure rises to his feet, towering over the woman. He reaches for her hand and pulls her close. Massive wings, ash grey in color, expand from the man's back, their tips dragging on the stone floor, and fold around the duo.

Gabrielle shouts, "No!" and rushes forward as a muffled cry of pain reaches her ears and a thin trail of blood begins to seep out from beneath the tips of those dark wings...

"Hey! Wake up!"

Gabrielle started awake with Stan's hand on her shoulder, shaking her. When she turned in his direction he pulled his hand back quickly, as if afraid of what she might do, and she noted with dismay that his lower lip was starting to swell.

"I'm awake, I'm awake," she said, sitting upright. With another guilty glance in his direction, she asked, "Did I do that?"

"Yes, but don't worry about it," he said, touching his lip gingerly with one hand and laughing in amusement. "I should have known better than to startle you awake after what you've been through. You okay?"

Gabrielle nodded, then, realizing he was looking at the road again, said, "Yes, I'm fine."

"Bad dream, huh?"

"Yeah."

As a dream it was bad enough, but Gabrielle wasn't sure that was all there was to it. Like the vision that had swept over her in the hospital, the images she'd just seen had a sense of presence to them, a depth of reality that made her think she was seeing future events that had not yet come to pass. The very notion terrified her.

If that was the future, she wanted no part in it.

CHAPTER 17

ARLY THE NEXT DAY, JUST a few short hours after Gabrielle had crossed the border, a Catholic priest pulled up behind the wheel of a dusty black sedan outside the hospital in Juarez. He parked in the first available parking space, conveniently ignoring the fact that it was reserved for the handicapped, and then sat behind the wheel for several long moments watching the crowd gathered by the front entrance before getting out of the vehicle and heading in that direction.

When he reached the mob he began shouldering his way forward, pushing people out of the way when they didn't move fast enough and ignoring the looks that he received in return. A few thought to do more than just look, intending to pay him back in kind for his roughness, but as they raised their hands and moved toward him something made them abruptly change their minds. Maybe it was the clerical garb he was wearing or the sense of wrongness that wafted off him like the stench of a garbage dump on a hot summer day. Either way, it allowed the priest to force his way through the crowd and reach the front doors of the hospital with little delay.

Two security guards were waiting on the other side of the doors, a metal detector between them. Just beyond, the lobby was filled with more of the same crowd the priest had just forced his way through outside.

The priest didn't hesitate. With his arms at his sides he stepped into the metal detector, sketching a complicated pattern against his thigh with his right hand as he did so.

If either guard saw him do it, they didn't mention it as they waved him through and on his way, the 9mm pistol stuffed into his belt at the small of his back remaining undetected in the process.

Access to the elevators appeared to be as tightly controlled as entrance to the hospital; security guards where checking the names of those waiting for the elevators against a list of approved visitors sent over from the registration desk. The priest walked forward and, with another wave of his hand, passed through that checkpoint with a minimum of fuss and delay as well. Those waiting for the elevator chose to take a different one when he stepped aboard, leaving him to head upward to his intended destination without company or hassle.

Getting off on the fourth floor, the priest turned right and headed down the hall, watching the numbers on the doors of the rooms as he passed. A nurse looked up as he passed her station, but she smiled and looked down again when she saw his clerical garb.

He continued down the hall, a shark moving through murky waters with no one the wiser.

It took him a few moments, but eventually he found the room he was looking for. He knocked politely and then, when no one responded, opened the door and stuck his head inside the room.

It was empty.

The bed was neatly made and the room appeared to have been recently cleaned. All of the equipment was stored in its proper place and from where he stood the priest could even see a paper sanitation strip lying across the seat of the toilet.

It was obvious that this room wasn't being used, but was instead waiting for its next occupant.

The Miracle Woman of Juarez clearly wasn't here.

Frowning, the priest pulled his head out of the room and let the door close behind him. He turned, spotted the nurse still seated behind the nursing station, and retraced his steps to reach her.

"Excuse me," he said in a middle-American accent that was a far cry from the one he'd been born with in Somerville, Massachusetts. "Has Ms. Rodriguez been discharged?"

The nurse looked up at him and smiled uncertainly.

"Um...Rodriguez, well, you see..."

The priest noticed that the nurse tensed up when she said Rodriguez's name and he guessed that she was on orders not to discuss that particular patient with anyone other than medical staff. Before she could continue he leaned in a little closer, smiled, and whispered conspiratorially, "It's okay, I'm a priest. Anything you tell to me is protected by the sanctity of the confessional, you know."

He added a quick wink and a little bit of a mental nudge to go along with it.

That did the trick.

The nurse looked up and down the hallway, as if checking to be certain they couldn't be overhead, and then leaned in closer to him with a smile of her own, saying, "If I could talk to you about that patient, which I can't, I'd probably say that she disappeared at some point the night before last. Morning shift came in and 'poof!' found the bed empty and our little miracle woman gone, just like that!"

"Vanished, huh? And no one has any idea where she went?"

The nurse shook her head. "I certainly don't, but if you ask me some people around here know more than they are saying."

"What do you mean?"

Another glance around, then, "Her doctor has been acting funny ever since she disappeared. Funny strange, not funny ha-ha, if you know what I mean. Locking himself in his office, shouting at someone on the phone at odd hours; I'm telling you, if anybody knows anything, he's the one."

The priest nodded, as if agreeing with her logic. "And where might I find this Doctor—?"

"Vargas, Dr. Vargas. His office is around the corner at the end of the hall, fourth door on the left."

He gave her another sly grin, one conspirator to another. "Thank you, Judith. You've been very helpful."

The priest moved off down the hall in the direction the nurse indicated and found the doctor's office a few moments later without difficulty. He could see through the frosted glass on the door that the lights were off inside and a quick turn of the doorknob told him the room was locked.

No matter. I'll wait, he thought.

He gave the knob all the way to the right as far as it would go and then, when it reached its limit, he gave it a savage twist, nearly half again around. He was gratified to hear the metal inside the lock crack and pop in response.

The priest stepped inside, closing the door behind him.

# # #

Vargas couldn't believe this was happening. No sooner had he made the call to that arrogant asshole of an FBI agent than his prize patient up and disappears from her room! He'd spent half the night searching the building, to no avail. At this point he had little doubt that she had left the building. The question plaguing Vargas was whether she'd left of her own accord or if she'd been coerced into leaving.

As he unlocked the door to his office and stepped inside, he found himself desperately hoping it was the former.

If she was out in the city on her own, he might be able to find her and bring her back to the hospital before anyone was the wiser. She had little clothing and no money – he'd made sure of that – so he didn't think that she could get very far on her own. If he could find her before the FBI arrived, he could still see his way to getting that payday.

But if someone else had figured out how valuable she was, just as he had, and had come to get her, then she could be miles away at this point with no way for him to know where she was going. Not only would he lose out on the money for turning her over, but he'd have to deal with an irate FBI agent on top of it all.

That was not something he wanted to do.

He flipped on the lights and crossed the room, stripping off his lab coat as he went. As he hung it on the coat rack beside his desk, a voice spoke from behind him.

"Hello, Doctor."

Vargas whirled about, staring in shocked surprise at the man seated in the chair in the corner. The stranger was dressed all in black – shoes, shirt, and trousers – and wore a white dog collar around his neck signifying his status as a Catholic priest. He was young and clean-shaven; if pressed, Vargas would have put his age somewhere in his mid-thirties.

The doctor was not a religious man, but the nature of his work brought him in contact with the clergy on a regular basis. Sometimes they were a bit judgmental for his tastes, with all their holier-than-though preaching and suggestions, but for the most part he found that they were genuinely interested in helping those under their charge.

This man was...different.

Vargas didn't know what it was, but something about the stranger set Vargas' nerves to jangling just being in the same room with him.

When the doctor got nervous, he tended to go on the offensive but something told him that might not be the best option at this moment.

Instead, he said, "I'm sorry, I didn't see you there." He gave a curt little nod and went around to the other side of his desk, unconsciously putting its bulk between him and the priest. "How can I help you?"

The priest frowned.

"That's it?"

"I'm sorry?" Vargas asked, both puzzled and strangely unnerved at the question. *Who was this guy and what did he want?*

"You find a stranger sitting alone in your office in the dark and your only response is to ask how you can help?"

"Well...uh..." Vargas began nervously, "this *is* a hospital."

"So?"

The image of a cat playing with a mouse flashed through the

doctor's mind, but he ignored it, still trying to understand what was going on.

"So we help people here. I assume that's why you've come? To get help?"

It sounded stupid even as he said it – no, not just stupid, weak, which wasn't like him - but there was no taking it back now.

The stranger cocked his head, a gentle smile on his lips. "Quite right, doctor. I've come to get help. And you are just the man to provide it."

"Well, ah, good then," Vargas said, unconsciously nodding again as if that put an end to the confusion he was experiencing. He settled into his chair, tried to flash a quick smile at his unwelcome guest, failed, and finally settled for repeating his earlier question. "So how can I help you?"

"You can tell me where the Miracle Woman of Juarez has run off to, for starters."

It was a simple request. It was even said in the same, gentle tone that the priest had been using since he'd entered the room, but something in the nonchalant manner in which he said it made Vargas's blood run cold.

He tried to bluff.

"Last time I checked she was asleep in her room. Let me call the nurse and see where she is now." He reached for the phone, intending to call the nurses' station if only to let someone else know that he wasn't alone here in his office, but his hand never reached the receiver.

The priest jumped up, faster than Vargas had ever seen anyone move before. He crossed the room in an eye blink, snatched a pen from atop the blotter on Vargas' desk, and plunged it through the back of the doctor's hand, pinning it to the desk several inches short of its destination.

Vargas opened his mouth to scream in pain and terror, only to find he could not; the priest had reached across the desk with his other hand and seized him by the throat, cutting off any cry before it could pass between his lips.

With one quick yank the stranger pulled Vargas out of his chair and halfway across his desk, until they were practically nose to nose.

"I'm so glad you did that, Doctor," the priest said, teeth bared in a rictus-like grin. "Involuntary confessions are so much more exciting, don't you think?"

# # #

When the priest was finished, he stepped away from what remained of the good doctor and shook his head in annoyance. As it turned out, the man truly didn't know where his patient had gone. The most the doctor could tell him was that the woman, Anna Rodriquez, disappeared at some point the night before. He'd scoured the hospital for several hours without finding any trace of her before returning to his office where the priest had been waiting.

Worst case scenario, she had been missing for twelve hours.

A person could cover a lot of distance in twelve hours, the priest knew. Especially if properly motivated, as the woman no doubt was.

The priest knew that superior would not be pleased with his failure to find her.

He glanced at the bloody mess that had once been the hospital's Chief Neurologist. The man had told him everything he'd known; the priest was quite positive of that.

CHAPTER 18

D AVIS WAS JUST STARTING THE briefing when Riley slipped into the ready room and took a seat in the back. He nodded to the knights around him and waved a hand at Davis in the front of the room, indicating that he should continue. Riley traditionally ran the briefing, but the fact was he was tired, still worn out from the events of the day before, and more than happy to let his second-in-command handle this one.

"All right," Davis began, "we've pulled the short stick on a shifter take-down in the Allegheny Mountains of northern Pennsylvania. Intelligence tells us it's a standard wolf form that's developed a taste for young, female flesh. Four teenage girls have gone missing from the surrounding towns in the last month. All have been found a few days later, their bodies half-eaten and abandoned in this general area."

Riley leaned forward, studying the map that Davis had just put up on the projection screen. It showed a heavily wooded area centered between three small towns, with a small offshoot of the Alleghenies rising in the center. It would be hard-going, he knew; thick forests with little sunshine and low visibility. *Perfect hunting ground for a shifter,* he thought.

Davis continued. "An investigative team has linked the deaths to Leroy Wilson, a backwoods hillbilly who has a cabin on the far side of Dalton's Ridge. We've been tasked with raiding the homestead, subduing Wilson, and transporting him to Longfort for trial and sentencing."

A hand went up in the front.

"Stevens?"

"If Wilson has been linked to the murders, why isn't local law enforcement dealing with him?"

Riley nodded to himself. It was a good question and showed Stevens, one of the newer members of the team, was thinking things through. Riley liked that.

"The means of connecting Wilson to the murders is outside the perview of the locals and would not stand up in court as a result," Davis replied.

Riley translated the official-speak in his head. It was magic, not forensics that had linked the victims to the murderer, which meant it was a team of holy mystics that had provided the necessary information. Clearly not the kind of thing a Sheriff's deputy could use to obtain a warrant to search Wilson's cabin, never mind arrest him for the murders.

Besides, he thought, *a shifter would rip even a squad of deputies to shreds. Best the mission was left to those with the experience to handle it.*

Having answered Steven's question, and not seeing any others, Davis went on.

"The weather hasn't been all that cooperative, so we don't have any satellite recon photos of the target site. Information gleaned from the locals says that Wilson's location has one, maybe two structures, but that's all. Unfortunately, there isn't an easy way in or out. We'll be taking the Blackhawks to here," he said, pointing to a location on the map to the west of the target site, "and then hiking in overland. Emergency extraction is via chopper from the ridgeline five hundred meters to the north of the target site.

"First and Second Squads just came off-duty last night after being in the field for several days, so this one will be Third's responsibility, with Fourth Squad tagging along on the ride as back-up.

"Questions?"

There were the usual back-and-forth regarding rules of engagement and equipment draws, but nothing out of the ordinary and the meeting wrapped up fairly quickly. When it was over and the men had been dismissed, Riley walked up to the front of the room and stood staring at the map for several minutes.

"Something wrong, boss?" Davis asked.

"I don't know."

Truth was, he didn't. On the face of it, it looked like a typical mission, but something about it was bothering him. He stared at the map for several minutes, trying to give detail to his disquiet. The terrain was going to be difficult, but certainly nothing his men hadn't handled before. Same went for the lack of intelligence about the target site itself. Hell, half the time they didn't even have that much to go on.

So what was it?

"Did the briefing give any details about the evidence that linked Wilson to the murders?" he asked.

Davis dug through his paperwork for a moment and then shook his head. "No. Just the usual B.S. that doesn't really tell us anything. Do you think there's a problem? I can check in with the officer in charge down in Intelligence and see if they can give us anything more, if you want."

Riley thought about it for a moment and then shook his head. "No, we're good."

Still...

"I'm going to accompany Third squad on this one. I want to see how Bautista handles himself."

Bautista was the new sergeant in charge of Third Squad and Riley hadn't had a chance to see how he operated with the men in the field yet. Joining them on the mission would allow him to do so, while at the same time help assuage the uneasy feeling he was having about the mission itself. On the off-chance that things went sideways, he'd at least be there to help get the mission back on track.

Davis, however, wasn't convinced.

"You sure about that, boss? You just came off duty; you should probably get some rest. I can accompany them if you want."

But Riley shook his head. "Nah, I've got it. How are we doing on those equipment recs that we put in last week?"

The conversation turned to day-to-day logistics and Davis let it go at that, for which Riley was grateful. He didn't know why the mission was bothering him, it just was. And the best way of being sure everything went according to plan was to have him right there in the thick of it.

After leaving the briefing, Riley returned to his office, intending to dig into the stack of reports on his desk that needed reviewing. His attention, however, kept wandering back to the coming mission and what he considered to be a potentially dangerous lack of intelligence about their target. Knight

Commander Williams might have been happy to run out on the edge of things from time to time, but Riley's style was markedly different. He preferred to plan things down to the last detail; that way, if anything went wrong, everyone knew what to do and when to do it.

Truth was, he and his team had precious little to go on here. They had a name and a photograph of their target, but little else. No information about the place where he was supposedly holed up beyond the GPS coordinates. No information about whether or not he was armed. Riley assumed he would be – at the very least he would have access to teeth and claws in his shifted form – but there was a huge difference between going up against a man armed with a shotgun and one armed with an assault rifle. They needed to know what they were facing.

And then there was the matter of evidence. Riley knew he would feel a lot better if he had something definitive that tied this guy to the four murders. Not realizing information to the troops was one thing, but he was the acting commander for the Echo Team and his clearance certainly should allow more insight than he was getting.

He decided it was time to have a chat with the Preceptor.

"I'm a bit busy at the moment, Knight Captain," Preceptor Johannson said, as Riley entered his office. "You've got two minutes, no more. Make it quick."

"Yes, sir," Riley said. "I have concerns about this afternoon's mission."

"Concerns?" Johannson asked, looking up at Riley with what was clearly impatience. "Such as?"

"Well, for starters, can you tell me how we linked Wilson to the murders of the four teenagers?"

"No."

Riley frowned. *No?*

"Does that mean you don't know or-"

The Preceptor cut him off. "What does it matter, Knight Captain? You've been given an order to take down this clearly dangerous individual. It isn't for you to determine if the evidence is satisfactory or not; that's for those above you. Your job is to carry out your orders."

"I understand that, sir. But you are sending my team in blind with little to no-"

"Are you telling me your men can't handle it? If that's the case I can give the mission to one of the other teams."

For just a moment Riley was tempted to let him do just that. It would keep his men out of harm's way and would be one less thing that he would have to worry about, but when he thought about the men who would be taking Echo's place, his conscience wouldn't let him do it. He wouldn't be solving the problem, he'd just be putting another team at risk.

"My men can handle it just fine, Preceptor. I'm simply looking for more information."

"You've gotten all you are going to get. Now if you'll excuse me, I have actual concerns that require my attention."

"But sir!"

Johannson ignored his outburst, leaving Riley the option of trying to push his luck even further when it was clear he had been dismissed or accept what he'd been told and leave it at that. Given that the Preceptor had clearly been behind the effort to have brought before a tribunal less than twenty-four hours ago, Riley's choices was pretty limited. Pushing his luck would just get him thrown in the brig. Or worse. Better to prepare himself for the mission ahead and hope for the best then continue to argue and end up having to have someone else lead the team.

Without another word, Riley turned on his heel and walked out.

# # #

An hour later, he climbed aboard the Blackhawk helicopter that was waiting on the pad and gave the signal for the pilot to get underway as he settled into his seat. Like the rest of his men, he was dressed in black BDUs worn over a ballistic vest to protect him against the were's claws as well as any gunfire they might encounter during the takedown if their target offered up some resistance, which he was bound to do. Riley was wearing his communications rig but had his helmet in hand; he'd hated how it made him sweat so he'd only pull that on at the last minute.

Connecting his communications rig to the Blackhawk's intercom system, he checked in with his men and then, once he was assured that everyone was prepped and ready to go, he settled back to wait out the ride.

As usual they would be flying nap of the earth to avoid showing up on any civilian radar systems, so the two hundred mile flight would take just shy of two hours. That would put them at their drop point by mid-afternoon. The plan was to hike overland until they were in range of the cabin and then attack just after darkness fell. That would be late enough to give them some cover from the forest shadows but not so late that the moonrise would give them any difficulty. Shifters weren't dependent on the phase of the moon to change shape, Riley knew, but the later phases of the lunar cycle tended to rile them up a bit more and they were only forty-eight hours away from a full moon.

He pulled a topographical map out of his pocket and studied

it beneath his penlight for a few moments, looking for anything he might have missed the first few times he had done so. Despite his apprehension, the mission was relatively straightforward. Their drop zone was five clicks from the target site; far enough to prevent an early warning but close enough that they could make the hike without difficulty. Once they arrived at their location, they'd do a quick recon to decide the best way of taking down their man and then they'd do just that. Once he was secured, the chopper would return for a quick evac and that would be that.

Short, simple, and sweet. Just the way he liked such operations. *So why was he so jacked up?*

He didn't know and it was the lack of knowing that had him on edge.

Oh, stop acting like an old lady, he told himself, frustrated. *You've done this a thousand times and your men are all well-trained. They'll follow your orders, even if it goes to shit. Your worry isn't helping anything.*

And that, in the end, was the reality of the situation. His worry *wasn't* helping and it made no sense to waste his energy on what couldn't be changed anyway.

Leaning back in his seat, he watched the landscape slip past and tried to grab some rest while he still had time to do so.

CHAPTER 19

THE CHOPPER TOUCHED DOWN IN the clearing just long enough for Riley and his eight men to disembark and then, once they were clear of the rotors, it took off again, disappearing back over Dalton's Ridge in the direction opposite their target to await Riley's pick up call.

Bautista took point, leading the men into the trees at a brisk pace, while Riley played rear man to the group, making sure no one was following them.

The forest was thick, but the abundance of game trails allowed them to make their way through the trees at a decent rate. They kept conversation to a minimum, using hand signals when necessary to convey a change in pace or direction; they moved through the woods as quickly and as quietly as possible in order to meet the mission deadline.

Despite their rapid pace, the shadows grew long and the sun was all but lost behind the trees by the time they reached their destination, a grassy knoll overlooking Wilson's homestead to the east. Leaving the men at the base of the hill with orders to hydrate and grab a few minutes of rest, Riley and Bautista made their way up the hill, climbing the last ten feet on their elbows and knees to avoid being seen when they reached the top. From their vantage point, they stared down into the narrow valley that Wilson called home.

There were two structures; a log cabin of decent size directly opposite their position on the far side of the valley floor and a larger building about twenty-five yards to the right of the other. The second structure looked like a barn, but there were no feed animals in sight and Riley couldn't imagine a single domesticated species that could be around a shifter and not go berserk. A beat-up Ford Bronco that had seen better years was parked at the far end of the valley to their left and with the help of his optics Riley could see the faint edges of a narrow, dirt road leading into the woods.

Only one way in and one way out for a vehicle, Riley thought.

They had only been watching for a few moments when the front door of the cabin opened and a thin, stoop-shouldered man in boots, jeans, and a flannel shirt stepped out onto the narrow porch, cigarette in hand. He stood there for several minutes, taking long drags of his smoke before crushing it under his heel and returning inside.

Riley smiled; they'd found their target.

He sent Bautista to the bottom of the hill to fetch the others while he took his time eyeballing the rest of the area around the homestead for a few more minutes, searching for movement. By the time his men him at the top of the hill, he was ready. Together they slipped silently down the other side and made a beeline for the cabin.

Assignments had been handed out back in the briefing room so there was no need to go over them again. Riley, Markham and Johns would take the front door. Bautista, Christoff, and Kelly would take the rear. Tamarro, Cerce, and Bodine would stay on overwatch, guarding the backs of the rest of the team and making sure that Wilson didn't slip away in the confusion of the assault.

They hit the target with the precision Riley expected from his team, just as they had a hundred times before. Johns kicked in the door and then stepped back, allowing Riley and Markham to sweep inside, before following in their wake. The trio swept through the structure, clearing each room as they went, until they met Bautista and his team coming the other way through the back door. It didn't take long, given the cabin consisted of only three rooms; living area, kitchen, and bedroom.

All of them were empty.

Where the hell is Wilson?

Riley was about to ask that very thing when the sound of a generator starting up reached his ears. He stepped over to a window and looked out around one side just as lights bloomed to life; some in the main cabin where they currently stood, some in the barn, and some tacked to trees at various points around the property, pushing back the growing darkness with their stark illumination.

Riley didn't see anyone outside but it was clear from the sound that the generator was in the barn.

He had no idea how Wilson got past them, but it was obvious that he had. Who else could have started the generator?

Not wanting Wilson to get away a second time, Riley quickly ordered the team to converge on the barn and within moments they were making their second entry, in much the same fashion they had the first.

The entrance to the structure was a large, rectangular door

that slid from the left to the right on a metal track. Riley raced across the open ground between the cabin and the barn and set up to the left of the entrance, with Markham and Johns on the right. They paused a moment to catch their breath and let the other teams get into position. When Riley heard two clicks over his radio, signalling that Bautista was in position with his men at the rear of the structure, he nodded at Johns, who grabbed the door and hauled it open.

Riley moved in immediately, with Markham and Johns following closely on his heels. The Echo Team commander went left while the other two men went right, moving through the structure just as they had with the cabin, the muzzles of their weapons tracking in concert with their heads as they looked carefully about.

The first two-thirds of the building was set up like a horse stable, with a wide aisle running down the center and a series of stalls on both the left and the right. There was also a tack room immediately to the right of the entrance, and a tool room immediately to the left which contained the generator. The team checked each location as they swept deeper into the structure, but didn't find Wilson.

The final third was walled off with cheap lengths of plywood to create a separate room, complete with a door of its own. That door was slightly ajar, a padlock lying discarded on the floor a few feet away.

Riley's senses were on overdrive as he went through the doorway, Markham at his back, the two of them splitting in different directions as they entered, gazes flashing about in search of their quarry.

What they saw brought them up short.

At first glance the room looked like an apartment, with a

bed, toilet, and sink on one side and a small couch and older-model television set on the other.

A young woman sat on the bed. She couldn't have been older than late teens or early twenties, was Riley's guess. Her skin was gaunt from lack of food and sunlight and her long hair looked like it hadn't been washed in a week or more. She wore a clean nightgown, however, which showed where her captor's priorities were.

The girl cowered at the sight of them, drawing her legs up against her body and pulling herself as far back as she could get on the bed, exposing the manacle around her ankle that kept her chained in place.

This wasn't an apartment, it was a cell.

But Riley couldn't focus on that or the prisoner quite yet. There was still the issue of Wilson.

Where the hell has he gone?

Riley keyed his throat mike. "Tell me you've got him, Bautista."

"That's a negative. There's no back door or windows on this place. He didn't come this way."

Shit!

Riley glanced up, checking the rafters, but they were as empty as the stalls outside. He glanced again at the girl, wondering if she had seen anything. The door had been unlocked, after all...

As if reading his mind, the captive's eyes suddenly went wide and she began pointing in earnest at the couch while saying something in rapid-fire Spanish.

Riley didn't understand a word of it.

He keyed his mike again. "I need you on the double, Bautista."

"Coming."

Seconds later Bautista was kneeling beside the bed, speaking softly to the girl. They went back and forth for a few moments, before the sergeant turned to Riley.

"She's scared half out of her mind, Captain, so I'm not sure she really understands what I'm asking. She keeps saying Wilson went through the sofa."

Went through the sofa?

Riley turned to stare at the furniture in question, rolling the phrase around in his mind, trying to understand what she meant, then hurried over to take a look. The couch was secured to the floor with thick bolts and wouldn't move when he pushed or pulled on it.

Behind him, the girl rattled off something new to Bautista.

"The cushions," he translated, while she pointed in emphasis.

Grabbing the closest one, Riley tried to lift it up, only to find that he could not. Kneeling down, he took a closer look, discovering the cushions were secured to a piece of plywood running the length of the couch. He found a finger-sized hole in the wood near the center of the couch and inside that, a small latch. Pressing on the latch caused the wood, cushions and all, to spring open, revealing an opening beneath.

Through the couch, indeed!

Since he wasn't immediately shot when the panel swung open, Riley figured it was safe enough to take a look. He drew his maglight from his belt and shined it into the opening, revealing a ladder leading to the floor of a tunnel directly below.

Stripping off his helmet, Riley held it by the chin strap and lowered it into the opening in front of him. When it wasn't shot immediately out of his grasp, he figured Wilson hadn't waited around for them to follow. He pulled his helmet back up, slipped it back on his head, and descended the ladder as expeditiously as possible.

The tunnel below was narrow and tight; Riley disliked it immediately. He shined his light around, noting that the tunnel not only ran back toward the cabin, but extended past the ladder itself in the opposite direction, away from the compound into the woods.

Escape route, he thought.

Before he could investigate any further, the sound of gunfire reached his ears from above. Riley turned and rushed back up the ladder.

CHAPTER 20

H E EMERGED TO FIND JOHNS hunched over the prisoner, working to pick the lock on the manacles that secured her to the bed. The others were nowhere in sight, but the sound of gunfire from the front of the barn let him know just where they'd gone.

Riley caught Johns' attention and then pointed behind him at the trapdoor. "Shoot anything that comes out of there," he said, and then ran to join his men in the next room.

He emerged from the back to a cacophony of gunfire. The short, sharp staccato sound of his men's weaponry was being answered by heavier caliber shots from outside somewhere. As he stepped into the main section of the barn he was just in time to see Tamarro stumble through the door at the front of the structure, an injured Bodine slung over one shoulder. Cerce was a few steps behind him, facing back in the direction they'd come from, firing at something outside. Bautista stood on the opposite side of the entryway, adding covering fire to Cerce's own, the sound of their submachine guns echoing through the barn's interior. Markham had the door in motion the moment Cerce crossed the threshold, sliding it along the runner until it was most of the way shut, leaving only a narrow gap between the edge of the door and the far side of the entryway. Bullets continued to slam into the thick wood of the door even as Tamarro carried Bodine into one of the nearby stalls and lowered him to the ground with Cerce's help.

Riley followed them in. "What happened?" he asked, even as he helped Cerce hold the injured man steady so Tamarro could cut away the cloth surrounding the bullet wound in Bodine's leg.

"Two trucks came out of nowhere," Tamarro replied. "Guys with guns poured out and started firing right at us, like they knew exactly where we were. We had no choice but to beat a retreat."

Tamarro began packing the wound in Bodine's leg with clotting agent and bandages, so Riley slapped him on the back in silent support and left the duo to help their comrade. Back in the main room, he found Bautista cautiously peering out the narrow slot left between the door and the jamb.

"Talk to me," he said softly as he slid up next to him.

"Two, maybe three trucks," Bautista replied. "They're parked facing us. I can hear men moving around out there but I can't tell how many or exactly where they are thanks to the glare. Cerce said they're armed with rifles and assorted handguns, though, so we're not just walking out of here."

Riley cursed under his breath.

Bautista nodded. "My thoughts exactly."

Any further conversation was cut short when those outside began hailing them with a megaphone.

"You there! In the barn!"

Bautista glanced at Riley. "You think he's talking to us?" he asked, a wry smile on his face.

Riley chuckled. *Leave it to Bautista to find humor in a situation like this.*

The voice outside went on without waiting for an answer. "I don't know which one of you is stupider – your commander for sending you out here to arrest me or you for following his orders. Either way, you're trespassin' on my property and I don't like that."

Gotta be Wilson, Riley thought.

"Out here in these woods my word is law. Far as I'm concerned, you've broken that law and wouldn't ya know it, in this jurisdiction trespassin's a killin' offense. So you've got ten seconds to drop your weapons and come out on your knees beggin' for my mercy or I'm gonna drop that there barn right down on top of your heads."

Riley nearly laughed aloud at the man's audacity. The last thing he planned on doing was turning himself or any of his men over to a killer like Wilson. Still, the man had a point; they were in a bit of a precarious position and they'd best find a way out.

And quickly.

The obvious answer was to use the tunnel, but Riley wasn't too keen on that idea. If it was obvious to him it would certainly be obvious to Wilson, especially since the other man had just used it to get away. There was no way of knowing where it led or what might be waiting for them at the other end.

Outside, Wilson began counting down.

"Nine..."

"Eight..."

So, the tunnel was out. That meant they could either use the front door – directly engaging Wilson and his men in the process – or create an exit of their own somewhere else.

Riley glanced at the men milling around outside, thought about the rifles they were supposedly carrying, and decided he much preferred option number two.

"Markham!"

"Sir!" the other man said, rushing over.

"Take a handful of breaching charges and set them up against that rear wall. I want an exit we can use when I give the word."

"Roger that."

Outside, Wilson was still counting.

"Six..."

"Five..."

As Markham disappeared into the cell at the back of the barn, Johns slipped out of the room and crossed to Riley's side.

"I've got the girl's chains off, Captain, but she's pretty weak. I'm not sure if she can make it on her own if we have to make a run for it."

Riley nodded. "I'm putting her under your supervision. Do what you can to get her safely to the rendezvous point. If she asks, tell her we're a police task force or something."

Johns nodded and returned to his charge. Outside, Wilson was still counting, his men hooting and hollering in support of his steady countdown. Riley was about to issue instructions to his other men when a new sound joined the fray, sending a chill racing down his spine.

It was the howl of a wolf.

No sooner had the first call begun to die away that another rose to take its place, followed quickly by half-a-dozen more. Soon the human shouts died off entirely, replaced by the echoing cries of an entire wolf pack raising their voices together in eerie harmony.

Riley felt the blood drain from his face. He and his men had come here expecting to deal with a single shape-shifter. From the sound of it, they were now facing an entire pack!

Bautista caught his commander's gaze with his own and in the sergeant's eyes Riley could see a reflection of the fear he was certain was in his own.

Snatching a single shifter with an eight man squad was one thing; taking on an entire pack was something else entirely. They were in trouble and the two men knew it.

Outside, Wilson had apparently gotten sick of counting. His shout of "Four" was almost immediately followed by the count of "One."

"That's it," Wilson called out. "Time's up. Turn her round boys!"

With hand signals, Riley instructed the men around him to move to the rear of the structure. When Markham blew the breaching charges and opened a hole in the rear wall, they were only going to have a few moments to reach the cover of the trees before Wilson's men were on to them. The shifters were making a fair bit of noise right now, but it wasn't going to be enough to cover the sound of the blast and they needed all the time they could get.

As Bautista and the others moved to do as they were told, Riley looked out through the door slot again, trying to get a sense of what Wilson was up to. As chance would have it, he was just in time to see one of the pickup trucks back up and do a three-point turn, the driver no doubt intending to end up with the bed of the truck pointing toward the front of the barn. In the midst of the maneuver, the truck drove through the cone of light cast by one of the overhanging spots, revealing a military grade machine gun sitting on a thick tripod in the back of the truck, one of Wilson's hillbilly compatriots sitting behind it, hands on the grips.

The barrel of the gun loomed large in Riley's sight.

He didn't wait around to see anything more.

He tapped his mike, shouted "Blow it" over the open line to Markham, and then turned to run, hoping he wasn't already too late.

He hadn't take more than three steps before there was a shrill whine from outside as the chain gun's motor spun up to speed. The whine was followed seconds later by a thunderous roar as the gun began firing. Bullets smashed through the aging wood that formed the front of the barn and filled the air around him like a swarm of deadly insects as the gunner raked the weapon from side to side in an effort to hit as many of his unseen targets as possible.

An errant ricochet caught the back of Riley's ballistic vest and threw him violently to the floor. It hurt like a sonofabitch and he was going to have the mother of all bruises come morning, but at least his guts weren't splattered all over the floor beneath him.

Bullets were filling the air above his head, as the other shifters added their own fire to that of the chain gun, and Riley wisely decided to stay as low as possible, crawling on his forearms and toes the rest of the way across the barn until he reached the door leading into the prisoner's room at the back.

Thanks to Markham's efforts, a man-sized hole had been blasted in the rear wall of the barn, allowing Riley to see through and across the clearing beyond to where the last of his men were just now disappearing into the trees. He slid over the threshold and kicked the door shut behind him, putting another wall between him and the gunfire. He rose to his feet, intending on catching up with his men, only to watch in dismay as several men stepped into view from either side of the barn, standing with their backs to him. He watched as they shrugged off their clothing and began to change, their bodies twisting and contorting in response to the call of their beasts.

Within seconds, the men before him ceased to exist and standing in their places were several of the largest wolves Riley had ever seen. They raised their noses to the sky, howled in unison, and then darted into the woods in pursuit of his men.

All but one, that is.

A grizzled old veteran with ash-grey fur and a large scar across its snout sniffed the air and then turned, looking back toward the barn.

Their gazes met and in the wolf's eyes Riley could see the sharp glint of intelligence and a whole lot of anger.

The Templar captain didn't wait around to see anything more. As the wolf came rushing toward him, Riley did some rushing of his own.

Straight for the couch.

CHAPTER 21

RILEY REACHED THE PIECE OF furniture and the entrance to the tunnel it contained about the same time the wolf reached the rear of the barn. The Templar captain pointed his MP5 in the creature's direction and let loose a burst of gunfire, forcing it to take cover to one side of the make-shift entrance in the rear wall. That was all the time Riley needed. Keeping his weapon trained on the doorway, he reached out with his other hand, triggered the catch beneath the center cushion, and flung open the hidden entryway.

He caught a glimpse of the wolf coming through the hole Markham had blown in the rear wall but didn't wait around to take another shot at it. Instead he threw himself into the opening in front of him, letting the trapdoor fall back into place as he hurried down the ladder into the darkness below.

He heard claws clicking against the wood that formed the trapdoor above, followed by a snarl of animal rage. Riley was just congratulating himself on choosing a route that the massive beast above couldn't manage to access when a crash of destruction reached his ears and the darkness was pushed back by light from above.

Glancing up, Riley saw a massive half-wolf, half-man figure staring down at him through the remains of the couch at the top of the ladder.

The creature pulled its lips back in a teeth-revealing smile.

As Riley backpedaled away from the ladder, he let his MP5 drop to his side on its sling, and, reaching over his shoulder, drew his Mossberg combat shotgun out from the specially made holster strapped to his back.

He hoped the ladder would give the beast some trouble given its size, but wasn't surprised when it dropped straight to the floor of the tunnel, bypassing the ladder entirely. It shifted as it fell, flesh twisting and changing in the blink of an eye, so that it landed on all fours in full wolf form when it hit the bottom.

Teeth snapping in anger, the wolf charged straight down the tunnel toward Riley.

The Templar commander fired, the shotgun going off with an ear-shaking boom in the confines of the tunnel, sending a load of silver-laced buckshot into the wolf's chest.

The creature howled in pain, but kept coming.

Still backpedaling, Riley fired again, this time taking the beast full in the face.

The wolf stumbled and went down, sprawling in a heap in the middle of the tunnel.

Riley knew it wasn't out of the fight. Shifters had an innate ability to regenerate, healing their injuries in a matter of moments. Interrupting their system with silver would bring them down, but there wasn't enough silver in his buckshot to kill it; the only way he was going to be able to do that was to separate its head from its body.

He jammed his Mossberg back into its case over his left

shoulder and drew his sword from the sheath he wore across his right. He rushed forward, raising the weapon over his head as he drew closer, ready to deliver the killing blow, but the beast had other ideas.

As Riley brought the sword whistling downward, the wolf shifted, transforming the upper part of its body into the half-man, half-wolf creature seen earlier and twisting out of the way in the process. Instead of taking the wolf's head off at the neck, Riley's strike bounced harmlessly in the dirt. Before he could recover from the effort, the shifter lashed out with one massive paw, delivering a backhanded blow that smashed into Riley's chest, picking him up off his feet and sending him flying through the air to crash into the wall on the far side of the tunnel.

Dazed, Riley laid there, watching as the beast struggle to get to its feet. There seemed to be something wrong with its hind quarters; if there hadn't been, he knew he'd be dead already.

Taking this thing on in a head-to-head fight was a clear recipe for disaster. He needed another solution and he needed it fast.

Glancing around, he noticed that the tunnel had been hastily dug, recently, too, from the looks of it, as there was very little shoring in place that he could see. That gave him an idea.

Rising to his feet, he stumbled several yards farther down the tunnel, away from the light coming down from above and into the darkness. He had no doubt the beast could still see him, but it was cover he was after but distance. He didn't want to be right next to the thing when he put his plan into action.

The shifter snarled in rage and frustration as it vainly tried to get to its feet. Riley ignored it, focused on the task in front of him. Sheathing his sword, he pulled two flashbangs off the clips on his belt. He hesitated for a moment and then added a third for good measure. He was only going to get one chance at this after all.

Flashbangs were designed to disable targets through a combination of concussive force and piercing light, overwhelming the target's senses long enough for military or law enforcement forces to move in. Riley had used them that way countless times, but right now he had another idea in mind.

A glance showed him that the shifter had given up trying to get its legs to work and was now using its great arms to pull itself across the floor of the tunnel in Riley's direction. If this didn't work, Riley was going to be in some serious trouble.

It's going to work. It has to.

Holding the flashbangs in one hand, he used the other to pull the pins and then quickly set them all down together against the edge of the tunnel wall, hoping the confined space would amplify their concussive effect.

With a final glance at the shifter still dragging itself toward him, Riley turned and ran into the darkness, keeping one hand against the wall as a guide and counting silently in his head as he went.

One one thousand...

Two one thousand...

On three he stopped and knelt quickly to the ground. Opening his mouth as wide as he could to equalize the pressure, he covered his ears with his hands and squeezed his eyes shut.

The flashbangs went off behind him, the blast shaking the tunnel and filling it with blinding light that he could see even through his eyelids. Right on its heels came another, louder, deeper, rumbling and the tunnel around him began to shake and pitch so badly that he thought it was going to come down upon his head. If the floor hadn't been moving so much he would have tried to hurry forward, but as it was he was forced to just hold on and ride it out.

Seconds later it was over.

Riley spun about, praying he wouldn't find the shifter standing there behind him and breathed a sigh of relief at the sight of the wall of solid earth that now filled the tunnel behind him from floor to ceiling.

There was no way the shifter was getting through that!

Riley climbed shakily to his feet, dusted himself off, and pulled the maglight off his belt. At first it wouldn't work, but after resorting to the age-old method of fixing electronics by hitting them a few times with the heel of his hand, he got it to throw a weak beam of light ahead of him.

The red light, designed to keep from blinding him in just this kind of situation, cast a cone of illumination about fifteen feet ahead of him, lighting up the tunnel with its eerie glow enough for him to see where he was going.

As best he could figure, the tunnel ran straight ahead in the same direction away from the barn that his men had been traveling when he'd last seen them. With the other end blocked by his homemade cave-in, he had no choice but to follow this section out.

Let's just hope they finished digging the blasted thing.

Ten minutes later he came to the end and discovered, thankfully, that they had. A ladder led to a trapdoor fifteen feet above his head which in turn opened out onto a small clearing in the forest.

He clambered out, breathing a sigh of relief that he hadn't emerged to find a pack of shifters waiting for him, and then set off to find the rest of his men.

CHAPTER 22

MOVE, MOVE, MOVE!" RILEY ORDERED, counting each of the men as they ran past his position, wanting to be sure they hadn't left anyone behind. When the last of the stragglers passed him, he remained where he was, waiting with his weapon at the ready, knowing their enemy wasn't too far behind and intent on reminding them that the prey they were hunting had teeth of their own.

He didn't wait long.

Just moments after Christoff limped past with the wounded Bodine slung over one shoulder, the first of the wolves came into view rounding the bend in the trail twenty yards behind them. Riley sent a short burst from his HK MP5 in that direction, smiling when he heard the wolf yelp in pain as his bullets found their mark. It wouldn't be long before the beast's regenerative powers pushed the bullet back out of its body, closing the wound behind it as it went, but until then it would continue thrashing about in pain as it was doing now and that, in turn, would make its brethren more cautious in their approach. Every minute they hesitated was another minute his men could use to get farther away.

He sent another burst into the trees surrounding the wounded shifter, just in case any of its companions were slinking about in the shadows there where he couldn't see them, and then turned and hurried after his men.

After emerging from the tunnel, Riley had followed the sound of gunfire to where his men were hunkered down beneath the bows of an evergreen, firing at the pair of wolves who were trying to keep them in place long enough for the rest of the pack to surround them. Riley had spoiled that plan, firing on the wolves from behind to scatter them, and he had then gotten the men moving again, knowing that their chances of survival would increase if they could stay one step ahead of the pack.

Run and live, he'd told them and made sure they did just that.

Now, to his dismay, Riley caught up with them less than ten minutes later. The team was milling about, the confusion and fear on their faces plain to see in the moonlight. Bautista was on one knee, hands cupped around his flashlight as he studied his map.

"Why have we stopped?" Riley demanded, as he hurried over.

"Runway stopped," Bautista replied, jacking his thumb over his shoulder in the direction they'd been running just moments before.

The Echo Team commander pushed his way through the group to see for himself, only to stare in horror at the chasm that bisected their direction of travel less than ten feet up the trail. The earth just suddenly dropped away into a gorge that had to be two hundred feet deep if it was an inch and a good forty feet across. It was if some giant had slashed through the earth with his knife, leaving a deep furrow directly in their path. They weren't carrying ropes, so there was no way for them to bridge it, and a glance showed the cliff stretching away to his left and his right as far as he could see. They were trapped!

As he turned away from the drop behind him, Riley caught sight of dark shapes moving through the trees below their position and he realized that the situation was getting worse with every passing second. The shifters might be holding off for now, watching them, but once they realized that the Templars had their backs to the wall they wouldn't hesitate to try to take them in a rush.

Riley had to find a way out before that happened.

His first thought was the chopper. There wasn't room for it to land, of course, but if Riley and one or two of the others could hold off the shifters long enough, the pilot should be able to hover over their location and pull the rest of the team off with rappel lines. If they worked quickly enough, he might even be able to save the rest of the rear guard as well. The shifters weren't using any firearms – few actually did, preferring their own natural weaponry – so one man could conceivably hold them off long enough for the pilot to get the chopper and the men it carried safely out of reach, leaving Riley to do his best to slip away in the confusion.

The Echo Team leader wasn't a fool; he didn't have any illusions about his ability to get away from a pack of shape shifting wolves that could most likely sniff him out from a mile away, but that didn't mean he was willing to just let himself be taken either. He'd fight as long as he had breath in his body; that was just the kind of warrior he was.

But first, he had to get the rest of the men out of here.

He hurried back to the others. They had formed a defensive

perimeter and were staring out in the darkness ahead of them, occasionally taking a shot when one of the shifters dared to show itself for longer than a few seconds in the moonlight. Riley hustled to Bautista's side and took a look at the map, then tapped the communications rig he wore to raise the chopper pilot.

"Nightbird, Nightbird, this is Echo Actual, over."

Nothing but air came back to him.

He tried again.

"Nightbird, Nightbird, this is Echo Actual, come in, over."

Another moment of silence and then the voice of the pilot came drifting in over the radio.

"Echo Actual, this is Nightbird."

Inwardly, Riley breathed a sigh of relief.

"I need an immediate evac at..." he glanced at Baustista, then read out the coordinates the Third Squad sergeant relayed to the pilot. "Be advised our backs are to the wall and we are surrounded by angry shifters. No room to land, so aerial evac by ropes needed."

This time the silence went on for a few moments longer than before.

What's wrong with this guy? Riley thought, his patience wearing thin. *Doesn't he understand we're in a bind here?* He was about to repeat his message when the pilot's voice finally came over the line again.

"Negative on that evac, Echo Actual. I say again, negative."

What the fuck?

Not wanting the others to hear, Riley took a few steps away and replied, "What's the problem, Nightbird?"

"No longer on station, Echo Actual."

No longer on station? Riley couldn't believe what he was hearing. Barely holding his anger in check, Riley said, "Then get your ass back on station, Nightbird! We need an evac and we need it now!

This time the answer was immediate.

"No can do, Echo Actual. Been rerouted elsewhere. Will try to find you another bird, over."

Another bird? Unless there was one in the immediate vicinity, getting another chopper onsite was going to take hours at a minimum. They didn't have that kind of time!

He was furious. He wanted to shout and rage at the pilot on the other end of the radio, but he knew that wouldn't do any good. The man was following orders, just as Riley was, and losing his cool wouldn't do anything to help the men whose lives were in his hands. He needed to keep things in check and work out the problem if they were going to have any hope of getting out.

The radio crackled and Nightbird was back. "Got you a new ride, Echo Actual. ETA ninety, repeat nine zero, minutes."

Ninety minutes? We'll be dead by then, Riley thought, but didn't say it aloud. It wouldn't do him or the guy on the other end any good.

"Thanks, Nightbird. Appreciate the help." Riley paused a second and then, on a whim, asked, "Who retasked you, Nightbird?"

The answer that came back was less than helpful.

"Somebody above my pay grade, Echo, that's all I know. New contact will be Red Eagle. Good luck."

"Thanks, Nightbird. Echo Actual out."

Riley turned back toward his men, thinking that all the luck in the world wasn't going to help them. They needed a plan and they needed one now.

He glanced around, searching frantically for something that

could help them survive the next hour and a half, but unfortunately no one had thought to stash a fifty caliber machine gun under a nearby bush and the chances that it would start raining rocket launchers was slim to none. All he had were trees, rocks, and a damned steep cliff, none of which were going to be all that helpful.

Or were they?

The trees stopped about thirty feet from the edge of the cliff, creating a section of open ground that the shifters were going to have to cross in order to reach them, creating a near-perfect killing ground.

To their left was a rock outcropping that rose about twenty feet off the ground and was surrounded by several oversized boulders leaning up against each other. If they used the rocks as cover, they'd at least have a wall at their backs when the shifters tried to rush them.

It wasn't much, but it was something.

Luck be damned, Riley thought. *I'm getting them through this!*

Determined to keep them from getting caught in the open, Riley wasted no time in ordering his men to take up positions amidst the nearby rock cluster. He deliberately took a point in the center of the line, as close to the front as he could get while still getting some protection from the rocks around them. For one crazy moment he imagined himself standing atop the outcropping and shouting out Israel Putnam's famous order from the Battle of Bunker Hill, then he laughed at the absurdity of it. His men were professionals; they knew to conserve their ammunition.

Besides, he mused, he was pretty sure that shifters eyes were yellow, not white.

He was able to confirm his supposition as fact moments later when the shifters finally decided to rush the Templar position.

CHAPTER 23

THE GUARD POSTED IN FRONT of the Preceptor's office saw Riley coming from the other end of the hall and made the mistake of stepping in his way and raising an arm in a sign for him to stop.

"Hold on just a minute, Knight Capt-"

That was as far as he got. Riley never even paused; just delivered a smashing right hook that felled the guard like an ox with a single blow. Stepping over the unconscious man's body, Riley barged into the Preceptor's office unannounced, interrupting some kind of a meeting.

Johannson was inside, leaning over his desk while studying a map spread out across it. Three men from his personal guard were there with him and all of them looked up as Riley entered. Johannson's eyes narrowed momentarily, but he then turned his attention back to the map, wordlessly dismissing the other man and not so subtly telling him that he'd deal with him when and if he got around to it.

That was a mistake.

Riley wasn't in any mood to wait.

To say the Echo Team commander was pissed would have been an understatement.

He and his men had barely made it through the night. The shifters had attacked again and again and if it hadn't been for the protection of the rock outcropping behind which they'd taken cover, the Templars would have been torn to shreds. As it was every man, Riley included, came away with some kind of injury, and two of his men hadn't lived to see the arrival of the backup chopper that plucked them from the ridge just moments before they ran out of ammunition.

He'd come here for a reckoning with the person he believed responsible for the disastrous mission.

Riley moved quickly for someone of his size and he was halfway across the room before the three guardsmen realized he might be a threat. The head of the guard detail managed to get around the desk in time to intercept Riley but it did little good; no sooner had he held up his hands in a "stop" gesture than the Echo Team commander did it again, pulling back his fist and punching the other man square in the face, sending him tumbling over backward to hit the floor with a meaty thud.

Riley stepped over him without a glance and continued forward, his gaze locked on the Preceptor and his hands curled into fists. He reached the desk and began to move around it.

The other man apparently didn't recognize just how close he was to taking a beating, for he glared at Riley moving toward him and, in a stunning show of arrogance, asked, "Are you insane? I'll have you court-martialed for this!"

Riley was too furious to even register the man's comment. He was drawing his fist back, preparing to strike for the third time in as many minutes, when the two remaining guards grabbed his arms from behind in an effort to restrain him. The

Echo Team commander struggled against them, never taking his gaze off the Preceptor's face.

"You set us up, you sonofabitch!" he said, shaking with fury and the effort to free himself from the other men's grip. "You knew there was more than one shifter on that mountain and you deliberately sent my people in unaware and unprepared to deal with them!"

The Preceptor glared back at him. "How dare you barge in here and-"

Riley managed to take another step forward, despite being restrained by the Johannson's guards, and the Preceptor took an involuntary step back, perhaps finally realizing that he might actually be in danger. A look of fear crossed his face, there and gone again in an instant.

The Echo Team leader barely noticed, too consumed by the fury racing through his veins.

"You sent my men into a trap and then left us hanging in the wind without transport to get us out of there. I checked the logs! It was you! You ordered our chopper to leave us there and I lost two good men as a result!"

Riley trailed off, too consumed by fury to continue.

Now that he understood what his combat team leader was talking about, the Preceptor seemed to have regained his composure.

"Now you listen to me, you addle-brained idiot," Johannson said. "You're right; I did pull that chopper. I needed it to deal with a pack of harpies that decided tonight was the night to suddenly start hunting the skies over Greenwich. I assumed you could handle a simple track-and-arrest."

"Simple, my ass!" Riley snarled back. "There was an entire pack of shifters on that mountain and someone tipped them off that we were coming. We were sitting ducks from the moment we arrived!"

The Preceptor waved the accusation away with the flick of a hand. "Perhaps before accusing anyone else, you should look to the men in your own unit," he said with more than a hint of derision. "They had more information about the mission than anyone else, aside from you!"

The accusation only angered Riley further. "What?!" he cried, struggling to free himself. "You stupid sonofabitch! I'm going to rip your damn..."

Riley didn't get any further.

"Get him out of here!" the Preceptor ordered. "Throw him in the brig for a few days until he calms down!"

It took all three of the the Preceptor's guards, but they managed to drag Riley out, still cursing and vowing that he'd see to it that the Preceptor would pay for what he'd done.

# # #

Riley had been cooling his heels in his cell for a couple of hours, a position he wasn't entirely unfamiliar with, when a voice spoke out of the darkness at the back of the adjacent cell.

"Seems you and Commander Williams have something in common."

Riley started in surprise and then watched as a familiar figure moved out of the shadows to stand at the edge of the light.

It was Seneschal Ferguson.

Where the hell had he come from? Riley wondered. The cell was empty moments before, he was sure of it, and he hadn't heard or seen anyone enter the cell block for over an hour.

"Yeah, what's that?" he asked absently, while turning the

question of the Seneschal's sudden appearance over in his mind. He remembered the secret tunnels the Seneschal had shown him that honeycombed the walls of the Templar headquarters in Rosslyn, Scotland. Maybe all Templar commanderies have something similar?

"You both have a remarkable distaste for Preceptor Johannson."

Riley scowled. "That's because the man's a class one asshole. He's lucky I didn't break his neck."

He was still pissed; no one had the right to put his men in harm's way unnecessarily.

It was only after the words were out of his mouth that he realized it probably wasn't a good idea to threaten the life of a superior officer to another, even higher ranking officer. That was the kind of thing that could get him court-martialed. Given the present state of the Order, it could just as easily get him shot for treason.

He waited for the Seneschal to reprimand him for such talk, but the reprimand never came. Instead, Ferguson cocked his head to one side and asked, "What has the man done to warrant that severe a reaction?"

Riley laughed, but there was no humor in it. "What hasn't he done?" he said. "His personal vendetta against Commander Williams cost us one of the most brilliant and effective knights I've had the pleasure of serving with; something the whole Order should be up in arms about. And now the men in the field are having their lives put at risk unnecessarily to feed what I can only imagine are the man's personal ambitions!"

At the Seneschal's insistence, Riley went on to detail how he and his men had been sent after a target with shoddy intelligence and then abandoned onsite for hours because the transports assigned to the mission had been rerouted elsewhere on the Preceptor's orders.

"Two of my men paid the price for that man's interference and that's simply not acceptable. The men in the field need to know that they'll be supported properly or before long they'll be finding excuses not to go out!"

Ferguson nodded. "When you put it that way, I couldn't agree more, Captain. I'll bring the matter to the Grand Master himself without delay, I assure you."

The Seneschal was silent a moment and then he asked, "Where do you think he is?"

Riley was confused. "The Grand Master?"

"No, Commander Williams."

He didn't know why, but all of a sudden the hair on the back of Riley's neck stood on end. On the face of it, it seemed a relatively innocuous question – after all, it had been Riley himself who had brought up the fact that Cade had been driven from the Order by the Preceptor's actions – but something in the way Ferguson asked the question had Riley's subconscious sounding the alarm.

In as nonchalant a tone as he could manage, Riley said, "I don't know."

Ferguson scoffed. "Come now, Captain. Do you honestly expect me to believe that? You were Williams' right hand man for years. If anyone knows where he is, it would be you."

"Ordinarily I'd agree with you, Seneschal, but I haven't seen him since the night we fought and defeated the Adversary."

"He just vanished into thin air? Hasn't tried to call or text you? I find that hard to believe."

I don't care what you believe or don't believe, Riley thought, his discomfort at the Seneschal's sudden interest in Cade increasing. He was struck by the distinct feeling that the Seneschal's only reason for being here was to locate Cade.

Was he in league with the Preceptor, too?

On the surface, it sounded ludicrous. After all, it had been the Seneschal who both helped Riley free Cade from the dungeons beneath Rosslyn Castle and had provided the money, IDs, and airline tickets they'd needed to get safely out of Scotland and on their way back to the United States. Ferguson was one of the good guys and the notion that he had so utterly reversed his allegiance in so short a time frame seemed crazy to Riley.

And yet...

And yet every fiber of his being was screaming at him that something wasn't right, that the man in front of him was not the same man that he had last seen deep beneath the stones of Rosslyn Castle.

Tread carefully, a voice in the back of his mind told him and Riley had every intention of listening to it.

"I assure you, Seneschal. If I knew where Knight Commander Williams was, I would tell you. I want to find him as much as the next man. We need leaders of his caliber now more than ever."

Ferguson nodded. "I agree. For the first time in a long while the Order is in a precarious position and it would certainly behoove us to have our best available when we need them. You'll let me know if you hear from him, yes?"

Riley forced a smile. "Of course, Seneschal."

"Good." The Seneschal paused a moment, as if gathering his thoughts, and then asked, "Anything I can get you?"

"Well, you could get me out of here for starters," Riley said, unable to keep the hopeful tone from his voice.

The Seneschal, however, was unswayed by his tone or request. "Sorry, Knight Captain. I can't, unfortunately, be seen to be playing favorites and you *did* strike the Preceptor's guards, after all. What is that saying you American's have? Don't do the crime if you can't do the time?"

Riley kept the smile frozen on his face as he said, "You got it in one, Seneschal."

"Good. I'll keep my eye on your team until your seventy-two hours are up. In the meantime, remember what I said. I need to get in touch with Commander Williams, so if you hear from him..."

"...let you know immediately. Understood, sir."

Ferguson stepped out of the neighboring cell, gave Riley a curt nod, and then walked to the end of the cell block and disappeared out the door without another word, leaving Riley to stare in his wake, wondering just what the heck was going on.

CHAPTER 24

HALF AN HOUR LATER, SENESCHAL Ferguson paced the confines of his office and considered his next move. His little chat with Knight Captain Riley hadn't been as productive as he'd hoped; the veteran had seemed to become more reticent as the discussion went on, almost as if he suspected something. Ferguson didn't see how that was possible, given that there was no external indication that anything about him had changed, but perhaps the Echo Team commander had simply been listening to those finely-tuned instincts of his and recognized that there was something a little off about "Seneschal Ferguson."

Either way, it seemed clear that Captain Riley could become a problem, just like his predecessor.

He needed eyes and ears in Riley's inner circle, someone who could keep him informed of what was happening so that if things did come to a peak, he would be prepared to deal with it appropriately. Riley's executive officer would be the most logical choice; he was involved with Echo Team's every action. But Ferguson was concerned that any change in – Dalton's?

Davis'? – behavior would be noticed by Riley and therefore become suspect. He needed someone who interacted with Riley regularly but not on such an intimate level.

A few minutes of thought gave him what he hoped to be the perfect candidate.

Ferguson picked up his phone and called the duty desk, where he confirmed the man in question was not currently in the field and put in a request for a meeting in his office an hour later.

His chore finished, the Seneschal went to make the necessary preparations for the meeting to come.

# # #

Right on time there was a knock on his door, which opened to admit the commander of Gamma Team, Silas Green.

"You wanted to see me, Seneschal?" Green asked.

"Yes," Ferguson replied, coming around his desk with a "come hither" gesture. "Please, come in. Have a seat."

The other man did so, but not without some obvious trepidation. For years the only contact between the teams and their ultimate superior had been Knight Commander Williams, so Ferguson knew Green was likely a bit concerned as to why he was being summoned now.

Wanting to put him at ease, Ferguson smiled kindly and said, "Care to have a drink with me?"

"I'm on duty, sir."

"Nonsense. A single drink in the afternoon won't hurt. I won't tell anyone, if you don't."

Ferguson poured them both a generous helping of Scotch and then walked over and handed one to the other man. He raised his own, toasted "Slainte," and took a sip.

Green did the same.

The Seneschal waved Green back into his seat and then returned to his own on the other side of his desk. "I've got a problem," he began once he was seated, "and I'm hoping that you can help me with it."

"I'll certainly do what I can, Seneschal."

Ferguson nodded, took another sip of his drink, which promoted Green to do the same.

"I appreciate that. I really do." Ferguson paused, as if thinking about how to approach a delicate subject, but in truth he was just wasting time, letting the alcohol and the unique substance it contained move through Green's system. "You're probably aware that Captain Riley was brought before a disciplinary tribunal the other night."

Green nodded.

"What you might not be aware of is that Captain Riley returned from a mission earlier today and promptly attacked Preceptor Johannson for some perceived slight against him and is currently cooling his heels in the brig."

Green didn't say anything, but Ferguson didn't find it difficult to pick up the man's growing nervousness and discomfort with the topic at hand.

"I have great respect for the Knight Captain," Ferguson continued. "His work since assuming command of the special mission teams has been as exemplary. But I have to admit to growing a bit concerned with his behavior of late."

The Gamma Team commander finally found his voice. "I'm sorry, Seneschal, but with all due respect, what does this have to do with me?"

"I'm getting to that, Sergeant. I'm concerned that the stress of the position is getting to Captain Riley. I don't want to see him throw away a very fruitful career over some impulsive act. I want to be able to step in and keep things from getting out of hand, but in order to do that I need to know what's going on within the unit."

Green was no dummy; he could read between the lines. He shifted uncomfortably in his chair and said, in what was more a statement than a question, "You want me to spy on him."

Ferguson smiled and waved a hand dismissively. "Spy? No, that's too harsh a word. I simply want someone I trust to keep an eye on him and to let me know when it looks like he might need a break."

The Gamma Team leader wasn't buying it. "Right. You want me to spy on him."

"Call it what you want," Ferguson told him, with growing annoyance. "Fact of the matter is that it needs to be done."

Green looked around, as if expecting someone to step out of the walls and take his place, and, when that didn't happen, reluctantly focused his attention back on the Seneschal.

"I'm not all that comfortable with that idea. Sir."

"Do you think I actually give a damn whether or not you are comfortable, Sergeant?"

Green didn't say anything, which Ferguson took as acquiescence.

"I will expect you to report back to me twice per-"

The Gamma Team commander interrupted him. "No, sir, I will not," he said firmly.

Ferguson stared hard at the other man.

"This isn't a request, Sergeant, it's an order."

"One which I'm refusing to obey. Sir."

Ferguson was surprised; he didn't think Green had it in him to disobey a direct order. Not that it mattered in the long run.

He'd already prepared for such an eventuality.

"Very well," he told the other man. "If that's the way you want to play it, you leave me no choice."

Ferguson raised a hand and sketched a symbol in the air, causing a small burst of arcane energy to flash between the two men.

Green's eyes went wide at the sight, no doubt recognizing it for what it was. Ferguson watched him try to get up, only to discover he had lost control of his muscles and smiled in satisfaction at the fear that suddenly blossomed in the man's eyes, like oil spreading across water.

Without a word, Ferguson rose and walked over to an armoire that stood in the back of the room. He opened its twin doors, reached inside the unit, and placed his palm flat against the back panel. A flash of blue outlined a rectangular panel that swung open when he removed his hand, revealing a recessed space about a foot deep. Standing in it was a jar of clear glass filled with a murky, green liquid.

Ferguson removed the jar and carried it with him back to his desk, leaving the armoire open behind him. He put the jar on top of the desk in full view of his visitor, savoring the fear that wafted off the man as he spotted the dark, sinuous shapes that were moving within the liquid it contained.

"I see you've noticed my little friends," the Seneschal said, smiling. He tapped the glass, causing the creatures inside to grow more agitated, their dark bodies flashing into view and then disappearing again just as quickly.

Green's muscles strained as he fought to move, but the paralytic the Seneschal had added to his drink and then activated with that quick touch of arcane energy wouldn't allow Green to do much more than twitch.

Ferguson gazed at the jar with admiration. "These, my friend, are conqueror worms. A bit rare, I must admit; they can only be gathered from the shores of the Sea of Sorrows and must be transported to this realm with extreme care. Not an easy task, I assure you. But once they are here, they are extremely useful creatures indeed."

He grasped the lid of the jar and unscrewed it with slow, deliberate twists of his hand, watching the Templar all the while.

Green's breath was coming faster, his panic growing, as he began to understand just how helpless he was. His face began to grow red with the strain of his attempts to shake off the paralytic and Ferguson savored every moment of the growing fear.

"Conqueror worms are not actually worms, you see, but rather psychic symbiots that can be attuned to a certain individual's mental wavelengths. When they are introduced to the nervous system of another creature, they allow the host to remotely control the victim's thoughts and actions, much like a puppeteer controls the movement of his puppets."

Ferguson's smile grew wider. "I'm sure even someone of your limited intelligence can figure out who these particular worms are attuned to, yes?

"Once one of these little beauties is released, it burrows through the victim's skin and attaches itself to the cervical nerve branch at the base of the skull, allowing the host to take control of the victim's entire nervous system. I'm sorry to say that the process is quite painful, but you'll find that out for yourself soon enough."

Having finished unscrewing the lid, Ferguson put it down on the desk next to the jar. He rolled one sleeve of his shirt to mid-forearm and then plunged that hand into the mouth of the jar, waiting a few seconds before pulling his hand back out with one of the jar's occupants clamped to the back of his hand.

The conqueror worm looked more like a centipede than a true worm, moving about on twenty-four little legs rather than sliding along the ground. It had a chitinous outer shell, two long antennae, and a double set of pincers growing out of either side of its mouth. When Ferguson held it out for Green to see, the creature pulled the front half of its body into the air and snapped its pincers in his direction.

"I think it likes you," Ferguson said and then moved around behind the chair Green was sitting on.

A high-pitched whine escaped the man's mouth as he realized what was about to happen, a testament to just how much he was fighting to break the hold the Seneschal had on him, but that was as much as he managed and far too little stop what was about to happen.

Ferguson didn't waste any time. He pushed Green's head forward, exposing the back of his neck, and deposited the conqueror worm on the man's sweat-covered neck.

The worm raised its head for a moment, antennae waving about, and then froze like a dog locking onto a scent. For a second nothing happened and then the creature raced up the back of Green's neck to a point just below his hairline and began to burrow its way into his flesh, disappearing into the blood-filled hold its pincers had created in the blink of an eye.

Green's body suddenly went stiff, like he'd grabbed a live wire and had 30,000 volts of electricity rocketing through his frame, and then slumped forward, limp and exhausted.

A few second later Ferguson felt the mental connection between them click into place. At any time he wanted, he could now look through Green's eyes, hear through his ears, even control his physical actions, all without the other man being able to do anything about it. Nodding in satisfaction, he walked back around the chair to stand in front of Green.

The other man's head was slumped forward, his chin still on his chest.

"Look at me," Ferguson said.

Green followed the instruction, lifting his head as if nothing had happened. "Yes, Seneschal?"

"Do you remember what we were discussing, Sergeant?"

"Yes, sir. You asked me to keep an eye on Captain Riley."

"And you've agreed to do so?" he asked, giving a little mental nudge as he did so.

"Of course, sir. An order is an order."

Ferguson smiled. "Very good. To be clear, you are not to tell anyone else about this request or meeting. You are to report back to me – and me alone – whenever Captain Riley does something unusual or beyond the scope of the orders he's been given. Do you understand?"

"Yes, Seneschal."

"Good. Dismissed."

The Gamma Team leader rose, nodded to the Seneschal, and then crossed to the door, pulling it shut behind him as he left.

The Seneschal mentally monitored Green's progress for a few moments as the other man began making his way through the halls, headed in the direction of the barracks, but once he was satisfied that the connection was solid and that it could be called up at any time, he let it drop into the back of his mind, waiting there until he needed it.

Not if, but when Captain Riley moved from being a nuisance to an actual problem, Ferguson was confident that he would have adequate notice to deal with the problem.

He turned, absently knocked a conqueror worm that was

trying to climb over the lip of the jar back inside, and then screwed the lid back on tightly before returning the jar to its hiding place and reactivating the ward that kept it secure from prying eyes.

Satisfied the issue of Captain Riley had been dealt with appropriately, the Seneschal turned his attention to what he considered more important matters.

CHAPTER 25

G ABRIELLE CONTINUED ON HER WAY, catching rides when she could, walking when the traffic, and the generosity of strangers, grew scarce. Slowly but surely she made her way northeast, headed for New England, guided by the few, scant memories of the life she'd had with her husband, Cade.

An elderly woman by the name of Eunice stopped to pick her up earlier that morning, stating, "We ladies need to stick together," with a seriousness that at first worried Gabrielle, but the widower turned out to be a delightful companion, if a little heavy on the gas pedal. Together they'd driven across Illinois and on into Indiana before she'd let Gabrielle off at a truck stop outside of Indianapolis.

Eunice, being the kind soul she was, offered Gabrielle all the cash that she had on her at the time and Gabrielle gratefully took it, knowing that $26.74, meager though it was, would at least let her put food in her belly for the next couple of days.

Eunice gave a little wave as she pulled out of the lot and Gabrielle waved back, silently wishing the woman well in the days ahead. *The good ones are going to suffer the most.*

The thought brought her up short.

Just what the hell did that mean? she wondered.

She didn't know.

And that's what unnerved her the most.

Shaking her head to clear it of her unusually gloomy thoughts, Gabrielle turned her attention to the truck stop behind her.

Unlike the others she'd stopped at over the last two days, this was no sprawling corporate affair but rather an eclectic little family-owned joint that was doing what it could to hang on in tough times. Wandering inside, the differences were soon apparent. It had washrooms, but no showers. Snacks and beverages, yes, but no racks of clothing or shelves of corporate merchandise. It did have a small coffee shop/restaurant, but Gabrielle avoided it in favor of just getting a cup of coffee out of the machine near the soda dispenser and Slushie device.

The owner of the truck stop had a trio of cheap computers and set up an "internet café" in one corner of the store. Usage was sold in fifteen minute increments at $5 a pop and a bright red LED display attached to every computer showed how much time one had left on their session.

Gabrielle was standing nearby, drinking coffee out of a Styrofoam cup and debating whether or not to ask one of the truckers in the store for a ride when a commotion at one of the computers caught her attention. A heavyset man in jeans and an AC/DC t-shirt who had been calmly video chatting with a woman a few years his junior suddenly lost his temper and began shouting at the screen. Apparently the woman on the other end of the call had no interest in being berated in public and promptly cut the connection, dropping the call. As Gabrielle looked on, the trucker swore at the blank screen for a few seconds and then abruptly got up and walked off, fuming as he went.

She watched him go and then glanced back at the computer.

The time clock was still counting down.

25:13

25:12

25:11

Gabrielle was walking toward the computer before she realized she'd consciously made a decision to do so. She sat down and tapped the mouse, bringing the screen to life. Tentatively, she began to examine the icons on the screen.

It had been several years since she'd used a computer and she was afraid the speed at which technology changed and improved would make everything unfamiliar to her. Thankfully, she recognized most of what she saw on the screen, including an icon labeled Google, and in just a few moments had the internet browser open and the search screen staring back at her.

Here goes nothing, she thought, as she typed her husband's name into the search bar.

Cade Williams.

More than 2 million responses came up. She glanced at the first few, but none of them had anything to do with her Cade.

Too wide, she thought. She put the words in quotation marks to narrow the search and ran it again. This time, the responses were limited to just over 17,000.

Better, but still too big.

A moment of thought and then she tried again, this time using a combination of phrases, "Cade Williams" and "Boston Police."

Her husband's photograph stared back at her from the very

first response.

"Hero Cop Gravely Injured; Dorchester Demon Slain."

Her husband's face brought back a flood of memories of that day. The Dorchester Demon was the nickname the press gave to a vicious killer that had plagued the city of Boston, never realizing how close to the truth they actually were. He had come looking for her husband and found her, instead. She remembered waiting for Cade to come home, waiting with that bastard's gun pressed to her head. She remembered the fear she'd felt, not just for herself but for Cade as well, and the sudden shock that had washed over her when Cade hadn't hesitated to pull the trigger and put a bullet right between the intruder's eyes.

She couldn't remember much of what happened after that, but that wasn't surprising given her shoddy memory. She still didn't have an address, but at least she had confirmation that Boston was the right place to start looking.

Gabrielle was about to turn away when the headline of a related article caught her eye.

"Cop Critically Injured; Wife Slain."

Heart beating in trepidation, she clicked on the link.

The reporter must have had a decent source, for he actually had gotten most of the facts straight. The writer noted that the killer known as the Dorchester Demon had fixated on Officer Williams for some unknown reason and had taken his young wife hostage in their home, luring Cade home by faking an urgent call from her. When Williams and his partner had pulled into the driveway, the killer had opened fire, wounding the other officer and leaving Cade to deal with the situation alone.

But that's where the story deviated from the one she remembered.

According to the reporter, Officer Williams had arrived too

late to save his young wife, who had been tortured at the hands of the maniac long before the phony phone call had gone out. The killer had strangled his captive and then used some kind of acid to peel away the skin from her flesh. One side of her face remained serenely beautiful, while the other was transformed into a ghastly ruin.

The picture the words painted were horrifying but even as she read them she knew that the reporter was wrong; it hadn't happened like that, hadn't happened like that at all.

Cade had come into the house and confronted the killer, that much was true, but rather than surrender his weapon as the killer demanded, Cade had taken a shot when the chance presented itself. Gabrielle remembered standing there with the killer's blood splattered across the side of her face as Cade rushed across the room and took her in his arms.

That was when the horror truly began, Gabrielle remembered.

Like a movie playing on an Imax screen in front of her, the memories drifted up from some dark, neglected place in the back of her mind, rolling out in High Def and Dolby Stereo for her to relive all over again...

...the killer, rising to his feet with that sick leer on his face and a bullet hole in the center of his forehead while she stared in horror over Cade's unsuspecting shoulder.

...the searing heat of his lips as they seemed to engulf one entire side of her face.

...the sensation of her flesh melting away, leaving her bones exposed to the light, as he pushed her away and turned his attention to Cade.

Just as quickly as they came the memories vanished, leaving Gabrielle gasping for breath in front of the computer screen. It took her several minutes to compose herself and when she did she discovered that her time on the computer had run out.

No matter, she thought. She had what she needed.

She would start her search in Boston.

CHAPTER 26

A FTER BEING RELEASED FROM THE brig, Riley returned to regular duty only to find that his mission status had been downgraded and that he had been reassigned to training duty until further notice.

It didn't take a Ph.D. to figure out who was behind the change in status, either.

He fumed when he saw the paperwork, but if he didn't want to end up right back in the brig, he was going to have to go with the flow and not cause additional problems. He'd had time to think and he wasn't just going to sit idly by and watch things deteriorate without taking action to protect his men.

When the opportunity arose, he called the leaders of the six combat teams – Alpha, Beta, Charlie, Delta, Echo, and Gamma – together for a video conference to discuss recent events. He waited until he could see the faces of the other five team commanders on his screen and then got right to it.

"Thank you all for coming. I know we're all extraordinarily busy, so I'll keep this brief. I'm concerned with the way things are being handled lately and I want to touch base with each of you to see where you stand."

He went on to detail the issues he'd been seeing of late, including an increase in the rate of supernatural activity leading to too many back-to-back missions, a reduction in the quality of the intelligence behind the missions being sent down from command, along with support and logistical problems like those Echo and Gamma had run into during the most recent mission.

The others agreed that things were far from ideal. They were exhausted and the end didn't seem to be anywhere in sight.

Gant, Charlie's leader, voiced a question Riley had long been wondering about himself. "What the heck is going on out there, is what I want to know! For years there seemed to be a balance, a kind of equilibrium between the forces of the light and the dark. Sure, we had our share of crises, but nothing on the scale we're seeing now. We've got a new problem every time we turn around. It's like there's something in the water, riling everything up."

According to the mission logs, supernatural activity was up by nearly thirty percent since the death of the Adversary. Now that didn't mean the two were related, but Riley couldn't help but wonder if something had been triggered by the fallen angel's demise. Were the other supernatural entities responding to some kind of power vacuum that the Templars hadn't anticipated?

Even that wasn't the worst of Riley's fears. He'd been looking at the numbers for the last few days and he was starting to see a pattern that was troubling. The veterans were seeing more than their fair share of the work, which, he supposed might make some sense. After all, if he were in charge he'd want his most experienced men dealing with the more significant issues. But when those men were wounded or killed in action, their replacements were coming from the ever-increasing pool of new recruits rather than promoting the men already in line for those openings.

In the past, the Echo Team commander had control over such promotions, but all that had changed in the wake of Cade's departure.

Like so much of everything else.

Those new appointments were directly under Preceptor Johannson's control, but given his own personal issues with the man he wasn't yet ready to voice his suspicions to the others that the Preceptor was actively trying to undermine the reliability of the combat units. He would definitely do so as soon as he had more proof, but for the time being he decided to keep his suspicions to himself and issue a more generalized warning.

"I want you all to keep your eyes open. If you notice anything unusual, let me know about it ASAP."

"Unusual? Like what?" Tyler asked.

"I don't know, Tyler. Anything that strikes you as out of the ordinary. Even if it's just a bad feeling in your gut, I want to know about it, okay? Dismissed."

He wrapped up the call, knowing he'd probably left them more confused than anything else, but it would have to do for the time being. When he had the evidence, he'd bring them into his confidence.

When he had the evidence.

CHAPTER 27

GABRIELLE WAS HALFWAY ACROSS OHIO when Death came for her a second time.

She'd been walking northeast along Route 32 since mid-afternoon, being ignored by every driver that came roaring past, and with the sun going down she was hoping someone would take pity on her and not leave her trudging along all night in the cold.

The sound of an approaching engine split the early evening air behind her and she turned to see a vehicle approaching. She stuck out her thumb, just as she'd done the last hundred times a car had come along, fully expecting it to go rushing past.

It did, too, the driver barely glancing at her as he drove by, but then, to her surprise, the car pulled over to the shoulder about fifty yards beyond where she stood.

Perhaps her luck was changing.

She hurried to catch up before the driver changed his or her mind.

As she drew closer she could see that the vehicle was an older model Cadillac, the kind that just seemed to go on forever.

This one was dark blue or maybe black, it was hard to tell in the dim light, and had dried mud obscuring most of the license plate.

The passenger window slid down smoothly as she drew closer.

Gabrielle bent over to look inside the car and in the second before doing so was suddenly overcome by an an intense scent of ozone, as if she were standing in a field and sniffing the air in the split second after lightning strikes a few feet away. It was there and gone again in an instant, so swift that she might have thought she had imagined it if it weren't for the fact that she'd smelled something like it once before.

This time she recognized it for the warning it was.

All of this passed through her mind in the space of a heartbeat, barely long enough for her to even hesitate, as she looked into the vehicle through the open passenger window.

"Need a ride?"

The voice was male and belonged to the young man sitting behind the wheel. Gabrielle put him at about thirty, maybe thirty-five. He was big; not fat, big. His hands looked like ham hocks sitting there on the steering wheel and his shoulders filled the space on that side of the car, making him seem bigger still.

Despite his size, he didn't appear threatening to her as she stared at him through the open window. He had a calm, jovial way about him, if the smile on his face and the tone of his voice were any indication. Just a good boy from a good family making his way home after work.

But Gabrielle wasn't fooled; not for a moment. For beneath that friendly façade, she saw another lurking like a shadow, full of dark hunger and twisted need.

Still, she didn't give any sign that she saw through his disguise.

"I do," she said, letting a smile of her own slip across her face. "Think you can give me one?"

The driver glanced at the road behind him in the rearview mirror and then back at her.

Looking for witnesses? Gabrielle wondered.

"Where are you headed?" the driver asked.

"Vermont," she lied. "Montpelier, to be exact."

Another glance, this time out the side mirror, as the driver seemed to mull it over.

"I'm going to Albany," he said at last. "I can get you that far, at least. Hop in."

With her hand on the door handle, Gabrielle considered the choice before her. It was a do or die moment, she knew. If she got into the car, she would be putting her life on the line, for this man was not who he appeared to be. On the other hand, if she walked away someone else would eventually be standing where she was now and their death would ultimately be on her conscience for not taking care of the situation when she had the chance.

This man was a killer; she had no doubt about that. The warning she'd just been given told her as much. So, too, did that inner voice that had been subconsciously guiding her since she'd left the hospital in Juarez, the voice that was telling her to get as far away from this guy as she possibly could.

She opened the door and slipped inside.

The driver's name was Jeff. He was pleasant enough for the first few hours, chattering on about this or that in an effort to appear normal. He happily paid for her meal when they stopped to get something to eat after crossing the Pennsylvania border, smiling all the while. Gabrielle had to give him credit; it was a good act.

His disposition began to take a darker turn, however, once the sun went down and they neared the New York state line.

"How was your meal?" he asked, seemingly out of the blue.

"Fine thanks," she replied.

Silence for a few moments, and then, "You know that meal cost me nearly ten bucks?"

"Did it?"

"It did. Ten bucks. And if you add in the cost of the extra gas I'm using to take you where you need to go…"

If he was truly going to Albany, which she doubted, he would have traveled the same route they had been taking all afternoon, so she knew his claims of additional expense were as fake as his smile. But that was beside the point. He was finally making his move and she was curious to see how it played out.

"Just what are you saying?" she asked, turning slightly in her seat to face him.

"Just that the ride, the food, they aren't free. They cost me money and I should be able to recoup my losses, right?"

Here it comes, she thought.

"I'm sorry, but I don't have any money."

He shrugged, still not looking at her. "Who's talking about money? There are other ways of paying."

Of course there are. And I'm going to make damn sure that you get what's coming to you!

She was quiet for a moment, pretending to think it over. When he finally glanced in her direction, she smiled coyly and said, "If you find a place to pull over for a bit, I'm sure we can figure something out."

The smile he gave her never reached his eyes.

Fifteen minutes later they came upon a highway weigh station that looked like it hadn't been in operation for years. It must have seemed a suitable location for whatever Jeff had in mind, for he pulled off the highway and followed the curving sweep of the off-ramp into the station proper. A small building that had once served as an office stood abandoned before the now-defunct scales and Jeff parked the car behind it, out of sight from the highway below.

Gabrielle let her right hand slip down between the seat and the door as Jeff turned off the engine.

Wait for it.

It didn't take long. Jeff turned toward her and his fist came rocketing out of nowhere, aimed right at her face.

It was a short, sharp, savage blow, no doubt intended to slam her head against the hard surface of the window beside her, the kind of blow that would take her out of the game right from the start, giving him all the time he needed to render her helpless and completely at his mercy.

What happened after that would not be pleasant. Of that she was certain.

Which was why she pulled up on the lever that reclined her seat the moment she sensed his arm moving in her direction, dropping the seat backwards with a sudden lurch that took her out of line with the blow. Instead of connecting with the side of her head, Jeff's fist continued past the point where she'd just been and connected with the window with knuckle-shattering force.

Gabrielle's would-be torturer let out a howl of pain and jerked his hand back into his lap.

In that moment, he was vulnerable and Gabrielle didn't let it go to waste. She sat up and, as he turned to glare at her with more anger and hatred than she had ever seen, she sent the knife edge of her left palm crashing into Jeff's exposed throat, crushing his windpipe.

With the damage to his throat Jeff had only seconds to live. Gabrielle expected him to sit there vainly trying to get air into his lungs as his life ebbed away and as a result was caught unprepared when he threw himself atop her instead, wrapping his hands around her throat and pinning her against the unyielding surface of the door.

If he was going to die, he apparently intended to take her with him as well.

Within seconds Gabrielle's vision began to dim and she knew she was in serious trouble. Her right arm was pinned behind her but her left arm was free and so she used that to hammer blow after blow against the side of her attacker's head, to no avail. The sound of labored breathing reached her ears, but she couldn't discern if it was her own or Jeff's.

She tried to twist and buck against her attacker's weight, to no avail. It was as if the presence of his own imminent death had given him super-human strength and nothing she did was having any effect against him.

Gabrielle could feel her pulse pounding heavily in her head as she fought for breath, willing herself just to hang on for a few seconds longer, praying that he would lose consciousness before she did...

Her right hand fell against the door handle.

With a surge of desperate strength, she gave it a quick yank and felt herself falling backward even as darkness swept across her mind.

When she came to, however many seconds or minutes later that was, she found herself lying half-in and half-out of the car, her back against the cold pavement of the weigh station parking area and her feet trapped in the car above her by the weight of

Jeff's unmoving body.

She kicked her way free,climbed to her feet, her gaze fixed on the man who'd just tried to kill her. When he didn't move for several moments it became clear that there was no longer any need to worry. He'd run out of air before she had and his body lay there, limp and lifeless.

Fuck you, she thought, as she raised one hand to rub her aching throat. *What the hell was it with people trying to strangle her to death? That was twice in less than a week!*

It was going to take some time for the bruises to fade, she knew, but better bruised than dead.

Words to live by.

Knowing that every moment she spent there was another moment that a state trooper or other law enforcement officer might come meandering down the road in her direction, Gabrielle didn't waste any time and got to work with single-minded efficiency that surprised even her. Grabbing Jeff's arm, she dragged him clear of the car and then, after looking around a moment, across the small parking area to the edge of the scrubland beyond. A drainage ditch ran parallel to the pavement and she rolled his corpse down into it, silently sending him off with another curse and the fervent wish that he'd remain there and rot.

Returning to the car, she took the keys out of the ignition and stepped over to the trunk. Inside she found just what she'd expected to find; a suitcase full of "souvenirs" from Jeff's previous victims. Just looking through it turned her stomach, thinking of all the lives the dozens of items represented. From the look of it all, he'd been plying his trade on the highways for some time.

That created a bit of a problem for her conscience. All of

these items represented prior victims who most likely had family wondering and waiting to hear what happened to them and she was now in possession of the only evidence. Of course turning it over to the police would get her tied up in the investigation into not only their deaths, but of their killer's as well.

She didn't have time for either.

Gabrielle pondered the problem for a moment and then made her decision. She closed the suitcase back up and then wiped down the handle and sides where she might have touched it with a loose rag she found in the trunk. Putting the rag over the handle, she picked up the suitcase and carried it over to the edge of the ditch above where she'd dumped the body, leaving it in plain sight.. Once she was out of Pennsylvania, she'd stop and place an anonymous call to the Pennsylvania state police and let them know what was waiting for them here.

It wasn't a perfect solution, but it was the best she could do for now.

Walking back over to the car, she glanced around to be certain she hadn't left anything behind that might tie her to the scene and then, satisfied, she got in, started the engine, and drove off into the night.

CHAPTER 28

SENESCHAL FERGUSON WAS WAITING IN his office when Silas Green arrived there at exactly nine the next morning.

Green hadn't wanted to come; had, in fact, done all he could to ignore the summons, but the thing living in his head hadn't left him any choice. When Green attempted to resist the mental command to report to the Seneschal, the conqueror worm played with the nerve junctures deep inside his brain, sending waves of excruciating pain throughout his body. After passing out from pain and being revived almost as quickly by the worm, Green finally gave in and went to see the Seneschal.

Upon Green's arrival, the Seneschal invited him in and directed him to take the same chair as before. Green showed no apprehension in doing so, which was good; that said the conqueror worm was still influencing the man's action. That would make the next step that much easier, Ferguson knew.

"It's time to report in," Ferguson said.

Green's eyes grew wide, but that was the only outward indication that he objected to, or even heard, what Ferguson had said to him.

The Seneschal didn't care. He didn't need Green's agreement for what came next.

Stepping forward, he placed his hands on either side of Green's head and called forth his power, linking himself through arcane means to the creature residing in Green's brain.

Closing his eyes, the Seneschal watched everything Green had said, done, and observed for the last few days flash past on the inner screen of his mind. When he came upon what he wanted to observe in more detail, he slowed the feed to a crawl, viewing the scene in near real-time. Most of what Green had witnessed was of no interest to Ferguson, but his senses perked up when he got to the meeting between the combat team leaders. He listened to Captain Riley's conference with annoyance and then swept forward through the rest of Green's memories before deciding he'd seen all he needed to see.

Green had fallen unconscious from the strain of the examination and Ferguson left him there, sprawled in the chair, while he pondered what to do with the information he viewed.

Captain Riley's suspicions were growing and that wasn't good. He had the potential of becoming a greater problem than Ferguson anticipated. Perhaps not as vexing as Knight Commander Williams had been, but certainly dangerous enough to cause problems in the days ahead if he wasn't dealt with expeditiously. It was time for Ferguson to put the next phase of his plan into motion; he'd delayed long enough.

Ferguson summoned his aide and directed him to take Green back to his quarters, then headed down the hall in search of the Preceptor.

He found Johannson right where he expected him to be, in his office reviewing the actions planned for the day ahead. After being admitted to the room by the guards outside – several more than had been there the day before, Ferguson noted with distain – he waited until the other man looked up before saying, "A moment of your time, if I may, Preceptor?"

"Of course, Seneschal," Johannson replied. "Please come in."

Johannson came out from behind his desk as the Seneschal closed the door and crossed the room, and the two men took seats facing each other in the arm chairs arranged before the fireplace.

"What can I do for you?" Johannson asked eagerly.

The man wears his ambitions on his sleeve, Ferguson thought with distaste, but managed to squelch his irritation before it showed. *Better to know what the man was thinking than have him plotting behind your back*, he told himself. Besides, ambitious men have their uses.

Like now.

He put an earnest look on his face. "What we're about to discuss concerns the future of the Order and cannot be repeated outside these walls, do you understand?"

Johannson nodded. "Completely, Seneschal. You have my complete discretion."

Ferguson stared at him, seemingly weighing whether he believed him or not but in truth just playing to the man's sense of drama, and then went on. "I must admit to growing concerned of late with the incidents the Order has been involved with. First there was that business with the Necromancer and the theft of the Spear from the reliquary. Then the death of Preceptor Michaels. No sooner had that been dealt with that Knight Commander Williams drags us into an unwanted and unnecessary war with the Chiang Shih, followed by all the problems with the

Adversary. One issue after another, none of which we were properly prepared for."

The Preceptor started to speak, but Ferguson cut him off.

"I wouldn't say this in other company, but I think the situation is clear. We've been living in the old world too long. Rather than waiting for the enemy to show its face, we need to be proactive in taking the fight to them. It's time we modernized how we operate. To do that we need new leadership at the helm if we're going to right this ship before it sinks completely."

The Seneschal could practically see the wheels turning inside Johannson's head as he tried to figure all the angles. He let him work it all out, already knowing what the man must be thinking.

Johannson did not disappoint.

"I agree completely, Seneschal. I will support your candidacy for Grand Master whenever you say the word."

Ferguson laughed.

"No, you misunderstand me, my good man. I have no intention of stepping into the role of Grand Master. I'm quite content right where I am."

He watched Johannson's eyes grow almost comically wide as he figured out the implications of what Ferguson had just said.

"You're not suggesting..."

"I am, indeed!" Ferguson exclaimed. "You're the obvious replacement. You are already running things quite aptly here in the United States and I see no reason those skills can't be put to the right use on a global scale."

"Grand Master Devereaux-"

"Is in poor health and I wouldn't be surprised in the slightest if his end comes much sooner than either of us anticipate," Ferguson replied. "You will have my complete support when the time arrives, which, I must confess, I hope is sooner rather than later for the good of the Order. Do you understand?"

The sharp glint of ambition was easy to see in the Preceptor's eyes as he nodded. "I understand completely, Seneschal."

Ferguson wanted to laugh; it was almost too absurdly easy.

It was time for a new Order to rise, one with a very different agenda.

CHAPTER 29

TWO DAYS AFTER THE TEAM meeting Riley was in the field with a bunch of new recruits in the late afternoon working on escape and evasion techniques when his phone rang.

"Riley."

"It's Gant. You need to get out."

Gant commanded Charlie Team, one of the other six special combat units in the Templar hierarchy, and Riley had known him for more than a decade. In all that time, he'd never heard him sound as scared as he sounded right now.

"Get out? What do you mean?"

Gant's next words chilled Riley to the bone.

"Grand Master Devereaux is dead. Preceptor Johannson has seized control of the Order, backed by the Seneschal. Warrants have already been issued for all of the team commanders. Word is Tyler tried to argue with those the Preceptor sent to arrest him and was gunned down for resisting!"

Riley was stunned into silence.

Tyler gunned down?

It sounded crazy. As a longtime veteran, never mind the commander of Beta Team, his loyalty to the Order should have been unquestionable and yet he'd just been killed by the very men he trusted most.

It was almost too much to believe.

And yet it was everything Riley feared would happen.

The sound of Gant shouting something to one of his own men shook Riley out of his daze.

"Gant, listen to me. I'm initiating Code Black. I repeat, Code Black."

"Understood," Gant said, "Code Black." He hesitated a moment, and then said, "Good luck, Captain," before breaking the connection.

Good luck, indeed, Riley thought.

Code Black was an emergency protocol put into place several years earlier when Knight Commander Williams was in charge of the special ops teams. It was designed as a fallback to protect elements of the Order in the wake of an all-out attack on the Order. Cade had been thinking of external threats, like those once posed by the Chiang Shih; no one, especially not Riley, had ever expected it to be invoked to protect them from their fellow knights.

Knowledge of the protocol was restricted to the special ops team commanders and their executive officers. Cade had purposely set it up that way and now Riley was very thankful he had done. The way things were going, it was going to get increasingly harder to trust anyone outside that inner circle.

Upon receipt of the Code Black order, the team commanders were to immediately scatter to the four winds, taking their units with them. Caches of weapons, ammunition, and other supplies had been secreted at various locations and each team was assigned to a different cache. Their orders were to resupply from their assigned caches, secure the rest, and then rendezvous with the other teams in the warehouse of an abandoned granite quarry north of Fairfield two days later. If that position was compromised, they were to wait an additional twenty-four hours and then try again at a secondary location, a safe house set up in Stratford, an old mill town northeast of the Ravensgate commandery.

Working to keep his reaction to the news off his face, Riley turned command of the exercise over to one of the lieutenants nearby and excused himself, hurrying over to the SUV he'd checked out of the motor pool earlier that morning. He was thankful he'd loaded his personal gear into the back before leaving, as that meant he had no reason to return to the commandery. Not that he'd have taken the risk; from what Gant had said, doing so would be tantamount to suicide.

Once inside the vehicle behind the tinted windows, he pulled out his cell phone and sent a group text to the team commanders and their executive officers. The text was a single word in all capital letters.

BLACK.

They would all know what it meant.

He just hoped he'd gotten the word out in time.

The cache he was assigned to lay in the hollowed out shell of an old freezer buried two feet below the surface of the ground next to converted barn Cade had made into a workroom. It was a forty-five minute drive from where he was, which meant he'd be arriving in the waning light of late afternoon.

Good, he thought. *Cade's house is pretty remote, but the less chance of being seen, the better.*

He put the car in drive and got out of there without a

backward glance.

CHAPTER 30

G ABRIELLE NEVER MADE IT TO Boston.

The closer she got, the more she became convinced that Boston wasn't the destination she was seeking. By the time she crossed the Connecticut border every fiber of her being seemed to be pointing her toward a little town called Willow Grove.

Since she'd come this far on little more than a whisper and a prayer, she needed to pay attention to her instincts.

The house was set back away from the road, barely visible through the trees. She would have missed it, would have driven right on past the narrow drive, if it hadn't been for that strange intuition that had been her companion since leaving the hospital in Juarez. That inner voice shouted at her to turn at the last second and she obeyed without giving it a moment's thought, jamming the wheel hard to the left to find herself on a partially overgrown track that led through the trees.

Gabrielle parked the car at the top of the drive and got out. She stood there for a moment, staring at the place her husband called home. It seemed familiar and yet wasn't. She felt anxious for the first time since setting out on this odyssey, wondering what she would find when she knocked on that door. Years had passed since her death at the hands of the Dorchester Demon and she had no idea what Cade had been doing since. *Would he welcome her after all this time? Would he even believe she was who she said she was, given the gaps in her memory and the fact that she was wearing someone else's body like a suit of secondhand clothes?*

The building was a solid-looking single-story structure with a wide porch stretching along the front. The late afternoon sun had already set behind the trees in the back of the house, sending shadows across the yard, but there were no lights on inside. Even worse, the place had that feeling of emptiness a house gets when unoccupied for some time, a sense of abandonment if you will, as if the very walls were pining for someone, anyone, to come home.

Cade wasn't here; she could feel it in her bones.

Still, she hadn't driven all this way just to be turned back by a few empty-looking windows. She headed up the walk and mounted the steps onto the porch. Autumn leaves had piled up in the corners; further evidence that no one had been there for several weeks. The blinds were down on all of the windows at the front of the house, preventing her from looking inside. On a whim, she decided to walk around back.

The first sight that greeted her was a large, two-story wooden barn at the back of the property. A path had been worn in the grass, leading from the back door of the house to the entrance of the barn, marking it as a place Cade had spent a fair bit of time. Her curiosity aroused, she started toward it, only to stop in her tracks when she happened to glance to her left.

A large elm dominated that side of the yard, midway

between the house and the barn. Standing in the shadows beneath the trees' sheltering boughs was a headstone.

A chill ran up her spine at the sight of it.

She turned and walked in that direction, a sudden suspicion blossoming in her mind. From this distance she could tell that the stone was new, the edges crisp and straight, as yet unworn by the harsh New England weather, and as she drew closer she could make out the word BELOVED etched deep into its surface. Beneath that was a quote from the Dickens' novel, A Tale of Two Cities, the final words of the character Sydney Carlton as he waited for his death at the guillotine.

It was her favorite quote from her favorite novel and it didn't take a genius to recognize that she was staring at her own gravestone. For one dizzying moment, she wondered if her real body lay resting quietly in the cold earth beneath her feet, and then she pushed the thought away, too unnerved by it to contemplate it further.

Unnerved or not, she couldn't escape the fact that for her husband and everyone else she'd known, she died on that summer day when a killer had come to call.

Poor Cade, she thought, knowing that the grave, as well as the headstone above it, could only be his handiwork. She doubted that she would have had the strength to go on if their positions had been reversed. He had meant the world to her and she knew that he had felt the same in return. Theirs had truly been a match made in heaven.

Until the day the devil had come to call...

With her heart threatening to break in her chest, she reached out and put her hand atop the headstone, feeling the need to connect with her missing husband in some physical way, even if just by proxy.

A flash of brilliant blue ignited beneath her palm the moment her hand touched the stone and a blast of arcane energy raced along her arm and enveloped her entire body in a dazzling display of power and light. She tried to pull her hand away, tried to break the connection, but the spell she'd triggered had been designed specifically to prevent that from happening until it had run its course and she was left unable to move, paralyzed and frozen in place as the magick hissed and crackled around her.

In that moment, she remembered.

Remembered *everything.*

The touch of the killer's gun against the side of her head.

The pain of the Adversary's power as it spread across her body, tearing her soul loose from her physical form.

The years she'd spent roaming the Beyond after escaping her captor, only to be dragged back to the Isle of Sorrows as bait for a trap when she thought it was finally over.

The shock of awakening in that warehouse with the Necromancer's magick coursing through her veins and the awareness that she wasn't the only one living inside her head.

The days spent a captive in her own body, her consciousness locked away in a corner of her mind while the Adversary wore her flesh like a puppeteer.

Everything that had happened from the day she'd "died" all the way up to the final confrontation between Cade and his angelic allies on one side and the Adversary on the other came rushing back like a sudden, surging wave that threatened to drown her in the tide.

And there, at the tail end of the flood of memory, was the knowledge that had set her on this journey in the first place, though she hadn't been able to recall it at the time; the understanding of just what the Adversary had done in those final few moments of the ritual that had been intended to destroy it.

Now Gabrielle knew the truth.

Instead of setting her free, it scared her to death.

When the flood of memories dimmed to a mere trickle, the power that held her in place finally released its hold on her and she fell backward, away from the stone.

CHAPTER 31

SOME MONTHS EARLIER, CADE HAD shown Riley a rarely used road that ran through the woods at the rear of his property. The Echo Team commander used it now, getting close to the house without being exposed to anyone who might be watching the property from the front. He parked at the end of the trail, turning off the engine and getting out. The woods around him were quiet.

Moving to the rear of the vehicle, he opened the back doors and lifted the floor in the back, exposing the equipment compartment that was built into all of the Order's assault vehicles. He ignored the various weapons stored in their custom-fit cases and grabbed the trenching tool from its place clipped to the underside of the lid.

Closing and locking the vehicle, he set off on a short walk through the woods that eventually led him to the back of the barn-like structure that Cade used as his workshop. Riley stepped over to the rear wall, found the small Templar cross carved into its surface, and then counted off twelve paces, the number of letters in Cade's full name. At that point he began to dig.

The ground was hard and the digging slow. It took him half an hour just to go down the first foot, but things began to ease up a little after that. At one point he thought he heard a car door slam out front, but when he didn't hear anything else he got back to work. Just shy of an hour after he'd started, he had the full length of the freezer exposed to the evening air.

He put the trenching tool aside and knelt down next to the freezer. A chain secured with a lock kept the door from being opened by just anyone. Thankfully Riley knew the combination – the date Cade joined the Order – and he quickly had it unlocked.

Inside were half-a-dozen long, black duffel bags. Each had been cleared marked with a tag indicating their contents; firearms, ammunition, rations, demolitions, water, and electronics. The bags were heavy and he was only able to transport them two at a time back to where he'd parked the truck. He had made two trips and was covering the freezer back up when he heard a sharp cry of surprise from the direction of the house on the other side of the barn.

Drawing his pistol, he went to investigate.

As he came around the side of the barn he spotted a woman lying in the grass in front of what was unmistakably a gravestone standing beneath the big elm tree.

The stone had not been there the last time he'd visited Cade's property.

Nor, for that matter, had the woman.

Something about the sight of the two of them filled his heart with trepidation and he had the curious sensation that this was the signal he'd been waiting for, even if he hadn't known as much.

Things were about to change.

Whether it was for better or for worse remained to be seen.

Keeping his gun trained on the stranger lying in the grass before him, he advanced cautiously. As he drew closer, he could see that she was Hispanic, maybe thirty years of age, with jet-black hair and fair features. She was dressed in jeans, a worn flannel shirt, and sneakers that looked a couple of years newer than the rest of her ensemble. She had no weapons on her that he could see and her hands were empty.

He slipped his pistol back into its holster and knelt down beside her. He could see that she was breathing and when he checked her pulse it was fast but steady.

"Hey," he said gently. "Can you hear me?"

When she didn't respond, he patted her cheek with the back of one hand a few times until she stirred and opened her eyes.

She looked up at him, clearly confused.

More confusing were her first words to him.

"Sergeant Riley?"

He stared down at her, stunned. He was certain he had never seen her before, positive that he didn't know her. And yet she knew not only his name, but the rank he'd held for a number of years in the Templar Order.

On any other day he might have suspected a trap, might have thought she was a wolf in sheep's clothing, some kind of supernatural entity wearing the guise of a woman in distress to lure him close enough to strike. But even as the thought rose in the back of his mind, he dismissed it, trusting his instincts, all of which were telling him that this woman was not a threat.

"Do I know you?" he asked, as he took her hand in his own and helped her sit up.

She shook her head, not in reply to his question but as if to clear it, and her grip on his hand suddenly tightened. Turning to him, she said, "Where's Cade?! Can you take me to him?"

Cade? he thought. *What the hell?*

"Who are you?" he asked her and her answer was perhaps the biggest surprise so far that night.

"Gabrielle Williams."

# # #

She watched his expression grow hard and his face fill with anger.

"Gabrielle Williams is dead."

She shook her head. "No, it's me. Honestly. I know I don't look the same but it's really me."

He stared at her, the skepticism clear on his face.

"Prove it."

"How?"

"I'm sure you'll think of something."

She had no idea what Sergeant Riley was doing here but she didn't have to be a mind reader to know what he was thinking. She desperately needed to make him believe her; he, more than any other person, would know where to find Cade.

Ten minutes earlier she wouldn't have even recognized him, never mind been able to answer his question. But now, with her memories restored, she had what she needed to prove to him that she wasn't lying, that she was, in fact, Gabrielle Williams.

She repeated the words she'd once spoken to him while Cade lay wounded at their feet.

"Names have power. With the right name you could even assault the very gates of heaven. And you'd have a good chance of forcing your way inside."

213

He stared at her, incredulous, and then answered her statement the same way he'd done so many months earlier when he and the rest of the Echo Team had been trapped in the Beyond during their investigation of the Eden facility. "So what are we going to do with that name?"

Her smile was bittersweet as she gave him the reply she given him that day. "You, Master Sergeant Matthew Cornelius Riley, are going to bind that angel with your bare hands."

"God in heaven!" he exclaimed in a stunned voice. "It is you!" For a moment he was at a loss for words, and then, "How?"

Gabrielle shook her head. "It doesn't matter. Right now I need you to take me to Cade. It's a matter of life and death."

He helped her to her feet and then delivered the bad news.

"I wish I could but Cade has been missing for several weeks now."

Gabrielle felt her heart seize. "Missing?"

"No one has seen him since the night he…" Riley faltered, unable to go on.

"Since the night he tried to destroy the Adversary?" she finished for him.

And stabbed me in the heart in the process. Oh, Cade!

Riley stepped back, the surprise on his face now replaced with something else. "What do you mean tried?"

They didn't know, she realized. The Templars didn't know!

"Look, I'll explain everything later but I've got an important message that needs to get to the Templar high command as soon as possible. Literally millions of lives are at stake!"

The Templar soldier grimaced. "Yeah, well that's going to be a problem, too. As of about an hour ago, the Templar high command is in complete disarray. The Grand Master is dead and a man I wouldn't piss on even if he were on fire has assumed command of the Order."

Now it was Gabrielle's turn to stand there looking shocked. She had no doubt that the Adversary was behind the problems the Templars were facing and it couldn't have come at a worse time. With Cade missing and the Templars close to falling apart, she had no idea what to do with the information she possessed. No one else would believe her, she was certain of that.

Riley hesitated for a moment and then said, "I managed to get word out to several of the other team leaders before the Preceptor assumed power. I'm headed out to meet them now. Why don't you come with me? You can tell them your story and we can figure out what to do from there."

It sounded like a reasonable idea and Gabrielle quickly agreed.

"We just need to grab some gear I left..."

Riley didn't get any further. From around the side of the house stepped a man clothed in the black clerical garb of a priest. He stopped a dozen yards away, his attention fixed firmly on Gabrielle, an eerie smile on his face.

"You've led me on a merry chase, Anna," he said in a voice that carried across the yard to them, "but now it's time that you came with me."

Riley stepped in front of Gabrielle, his pistol back in his hand. "You know this guy?" he asked over his shoulder, never taking his gaze off the newcomer.

"Never seen him before in my life but I can tell you I don't like the looks of him."

Riley brought his gun up and pointed it at the intruder. "Don't know who you are or what you want, but this is private property and you aren't welcome, mister. I suggest you get yourself back to wherever it is that you came from and do it *tout suite*."

The priest looked at him. "I'm here on orders of the Seneschal, Templar. Move aside."

"Yeah, not happening," Riley called out. In a lower voice he said to Gabrielle, "I've got a vehicle parked in a clearing in the woods behind the workshop. When I give the word start heading in that direction."

But before Gabrielle had a chance to take even a single step, two humanoid figures came swooping down from above and landed midway between them and the priest.

The newcomers were shaped like humans, if you ignored the large bat-like wings jutting out behind their backs, the jagged claws at the ends of their fingers and the smooth, featureless expanse of their faces.

Riley recognized them for what they were – nightgaunts, denizens of the lower planes – and realized that things had just gotten considerably more dangerous for him and his new charge.

Rather than being terrified at the sight, however, Gabrielle rose to the occasion. "Give me a weapon," she said from over his shoulder. "I can fight."

"No, head for the workshop…"

She cut him off. "I'm not leaving, you idiot! Are you going to give me a weapon or just leave me here to be gutted like a fish?"

Well, when you put it that way.

All Riley had on him at the moment was the pistol in his hand and his blessed sword in the sheath strapped to his back. He passed her the firearm.

"You know how to use that?"

"I'm a policeman's wife," she replied, as if that was answer enough.

Watching the way she checked the magazine and then chambered a round, Riley decided that perhaps it was.

The nightgaunts stood where they'd landed, their long forked tongues snaking out and testing the air. They hissed in Riley's direction, but made no move to advance.

The priest called out again. "Last chance, Anna. Come with me now and no one gets hurt."

In reply, Gabrielle brought the weapon up and snapped off a shot in the priest's direction, missing him by less than an inch as he dove out of the way.

With piercing shrieks issuing from heaven-knew-where, the nightgaunts threw themselves into fray. With powerful thrusts of their hind legs they crossed the space between them and their quarry in seconds, gliding through the air with the help of their massive wings, lashing at both Riley and Gabrielle with their impressive claws, before swooping upward to try again.

The Templar and his companion weren't without recourse of their own, however. Riley lashed at the creature closest to him as it went by, the sudden tug on his blade letting him know he'd scored a hit. Gabrielle turned out to be an excellent marksman and she put at least two shots into the body of her attacker the first few times it tried to attack.

Time and time again the nightgaunts attacked and each time the two fended them off. It didn't take long for Riley's arms to grow tired nor Gabrielle to run low on ammunition, but by then the attackers started to show signs of injury as well.

As one of the nightgaunts hovered above them, lashing with its claws, Riley changed tactics. Instead of slashing at it with the edge of his blade, he leapt upward as high as he could go, jabbing the point of his blade into the creature's abdomen and dragging it down with him as gravity pulled him back to earth.

Seeing what he'd done, Gabrielle turned and put a pair of bullets into the thing's skull, killing it.

At that point the two of them were able to focus all of their attention on the remaining nightgaunt. Given that it was injured, they were able to make short work of it.

Exhausted, Riley lowered his sword and was about to complement Gabrielle on her shooting when she screamed, "Look out!" and barreled into him, knocking him down atop the corpse of the creature he'd just slain.

As a result, the burst of bullets that should have taken his head off at the shoulders passed over him without injury. He lifted his head and saw the priest standing about twenty-five feet away, one of the assault rifles from the cache held in his hands and pointed in their direction. The priest was lining up the weapon to try again when Gabrielle's arm snapped up and she put a pair of bullets smack into the center of his chest.

The rifle fired wildly as the priest fell over backward, with none of his bullets finding their mark.

"Thanks," Riley said, as he fought to catch his breathe.

Still too pumped on adrenaline to say anything, Gabrielle just nodded.

Riley rose to his feet and retrieved the firearm from the priest's grasp. Walking around to the back of the workshop, they paused to allow Riley to retrieve the last two duffle bags and then he led her through the woods to the waiting vehicle.

CHAPTER 32

AS THE PAIR DISAPPEARED INTO the woods, a figured dressed in dark clothes and a hood stepped from the shadows near the main house. The newcomer stood watching the departing vehicle for a moment, then turned and walked across the yard to where the confrontation had just taken place.

He stood over the body of the first nightgaunt he came to and stared down at it, an expression of disgust on his face. He lifted his hand and held it over the corpse, palm down. There was a flash of blue light, there and gone again in a moment, and then the stranger moved on to the next corpse, repeating the process.

Behind him, the first of the nightgaunts began collapsing in on itself, crumbling away bit by bit until there was nothing left but a small pile of fine, dark ash. That, too, would be gone by morning, lifted and scattered about by the wind until there was nothing left to prove that such a creature ever existed.

He repeated his efforts above the corpse of the other, then turned his attention to the body of the priest. The demon that had possessed it was gone now, sent back to the Infernal Plane upon his death, and the body left behind was just that, a body, and nothing more. There was no need to destroy it as he had the others, for it wouldn't reveal anything out of the ordinary to whoever had the misfortune to stumble across it.

He turned and stared once more in the direction the Templar and his new companion had gone. Captain Riley might not have recognized the Nephilim's wife at first glance, but he certainly had, physical appearance notwithstanding. The years she'd spent in the Beyond were marked on her soul and he'd been able to see those marks shining bright and clear beneath the flesh of her physical form.

Her continued existence, even in a body not her own, gave him hope that all was not lost. He'd known for weeks that something had gone radically wrong with his former companion's plan to eliminate the Adversary once and for all and he'd spent the time since gradually piecing together the truth of what had occurred. That knowledge threatened to send him back into isolation, for he'd seen no way of stopping the cataclysm to come.

But now...

Now there was hope, slim though it may be.

The woman was the key.

With her in the forefront of his thoughts, he strode over to the headstone sticking out of the earth nearby. Just as Gabrielle had done before him, he ran his fingers over the inscription carved into the rock.

The irony was not lost on him.

His spell had worked, restoring the woman's memory so that she could let the others know what lay ahead for them. If they did not act, and act swiftly, their chance to save this world would pass them by.

The time for rest was over.

It was time for war.

With a final glance to be certain he hadn't missed anything, he turned and strode into the shadows beneath the trees, disappearing from view as if he hadn't ever been there at all.

CHAPTER 33

RILEY, WITH GABRIELLE IN TOW, was the last to arrive at the abandoned smelting facility and warehouse that served as the rendezvous point for the code black signal. More than a few of the men waiting inside breathed a sigh of relief at his appearance, which was the first sign that things had not gone as well as he'd hoped. Glancing around at the men gathered there, he received another sign; there were only twenty-five, maybe thirty men in total.

Less than half, Riley thought with dismay.

Things weren't going to be easy, he knew.

Quite a few of those assembled were staring at Gabrielle, wondering what she was doing there, and he knew he was going to need to address that question sooner rather than later. But first there were things that needed to get done.

He sent pairs of men to watch both the front and rear entrances of the building, as well as putting another set of eyes up on the roof. He had the team leaders report in, giving him the status of their men and the supply caches they'd retrieved, and accounts of what they'd run into in the process.

When that was finished, he introduced Gabrielle to the men as someone who could explain some of what was happening.

With that, he turned the floor over to her.

Gabrielle stepped into the space Riley provided, out in front of the assembled men, and looked them over, seeing the doubt and the apprehension on their faces. She knew that this was not a time for equivocations. She had come here to warn them and warn them she would.

"I suspect that some of you know the story of how Knight Commander Williams came to be a Templar," she began.

Several of the men nodded.

"The story of how the Adversary possessed the body of a killer and used that man to attack Commander Williams and to slay Williams' wife, Gabrielle. Of how Williams joined the Order to seek vengeance on the Adversary, to make him pay for the life he'd taken."

She had their attention now; stories about the man some called the heretic tended to do that. She gave them a moment to take it in, to let the tension build in a way that would get them to listen to what it was she had to say.

"I'm here to tell you that there is far more to that story, starting with the fact that Cade's wife did not die that day. I should know, for I am that woman. I am Gabrielle Williams."

And with that introduction, she told them everything.

Of her time spent wandering the Beyond.

Of her efforts to warn and assist Cade whenever she had the power to pierce the Veil and cross the barrier from the Beyond.

Of the days spent trapped on the Isle of Sorrows, only to be released when Cade sent the Adversary back to the Infernal Realm where it belonged.

Of the horror she'd endured as the Necromancer's ritual had

reunited her spirit with her body, only to discover that the Adversary shared that same space with her.

And finally, of what the Adversary had done in those final moments.

"With our minds and spirits sharing the same physical shell, the Adversary was free to plumb the depths of my very soul, to share my memories, to plunder my secrets. But the connection worked both ways, as I slowly came to realize.

"While he could see into my thoughts, I was free to see into his own."

Every eye was fixed on her as her story sped toward its climax.

"In that final moment, when Cade drove his blade into my heart activating the ritual he and his angelic allies had fought to invoke, I saw the Adversary's true purpose. The ritual would not destroy him, as the angels intended; in fact, it had the opposite effect. The ritual allowed him to channel his power in conjunction with those of his former scream that waited in the underworld. With that one final burst of power he and his allies possessed the angels before them, driving out the divine spirits and seizing control of the physical bodies for their own. Not only does the Adversary live anew, but he now has his six most powerful allies at his side!"

For several seconds the room was utterly silent.

Then a voice rang out from the middle of the group.

"I don't believe you."

Riley turned at the sound and saw Green, Gamma's commander, pushing his way forward through the ranks of the men until he could face Gabrielle directly.

"You come in here expecting us to believe a cockamamie story like that? How do we even know you are who you say you are? You could be just about anybody with an invented story, trying to infiltrate our ranks and throw us off our true mission!"

Riley could see that Green's words were having an impact. Several men were talking between themselves now, casting discomforting glances in Gabrielle's direction.

He stepped forward to stand next to Gabrielle.

"I have absolutely no doubt," he said, "that this is Gabrielle Williams. I would not have brought here her if I had any suspicions otherwise."

"With all due respect, Captain, I think you're in over your head. Your word isn't good enough for me anymore."

Riley couldn't believe what he was hearing. Green had always been a team player and this kind of insubordination was completely unlike him.

But before he could say anything in response, a figure stepped out of the shadows off to their left.

"Perhaps you'll take my word for it then, as she indeed speaks the truth."

The giant of a man might as well have just appeared out of thin air. Riley had looked in that direction earlier and he would have sworn that no one had been there. The newcomer wore a dark cloak and hood that covered him from head to foot, keeping his face in shadow, but power seemed to radiate off him in waves and more than a few of the assembled Templars hastily pointed their weapons in his direction.

The newcomer appeared not to notice. He looked over those assembled and then turned to face Riley.

"You need to listen to her," the newcomer insisted.

Riley didn't have any objection to listening to Gabrielle. He had, in fact, brought her here for that very purpose. After all, he knew she was who she said she was.

This stranger on the other hand...

Holding up a hand to keep any of his men from acting precipitously, he asked the stranger, "Who are you?"

The newcomer came forward a few steps so that he was no longer hidden in the shadows. Reaching up, he took off the hood that concealed his face.

"I have been known by many names through the years," he said, "but you can call me Uriel."

Riley stared at him, taking in the square-jawed masculine face, a face that was human and yet not, a face that was perfectly proportioned in every way, so much so that it appeared almost alien in its perfection.

"*The* Uriel?" he asked.

The man tilted his head to look at Riley from an angle, reminding him of a dog cocking his head to the side.

No dog was ever that powerful or dangerous, he thought.

"Who would pretend to be that if he were not?" Uriel replied.

Riley considered that a moment. He'd seen his fair share of angels, including the resurrected one, Baraquel, that he'd bound to his will, and he was willing to give the entity before them the benefit of the doubt.

Some of the others were not so easily convinced.

Green, still looking for an argument it seemed, stepped forward. "You expect us to believe that you're an archangel of the Lord? What? We're just supposed to take your word for it?"

Uriel glanced at Riley, his expression unreadable, and then he turned and thrust one hand in Green's direction. As if caught by an invisible power, the other man froze in place, unable to move even the slightest muscle. Riley could see the struggle Green was putting up in the depths of his eyes, but that was the only outward indication that he was fighting against whatever it was that held him in place.

Uriel watched him the way a boy might watch a bug under a magnifying glass, curious but with no real feeling. It was clear to Riley that Uriel would just as soon crush his fellow Templar as let him go.

Without looking away from Green, the archangel addressed the others.

"I am as old as time itself. I am the watcher in the dark, the chronicler of the ages. It is my curse to watch and record all that passes in the world of men in order to keep the balance."

He reached up and parted the front of his robe, revealing his chest. His skin was the color of burnt sienna, but it was the tattoos that caught Riley's eye. Every inch of his flesh seemed to be covered; from the base of Uriel's neck down to the waist of his jeans and apparently lower still.

The tattoos twisted and moved and roamed about on his flesh like living, breathing creations with a life all their own. Images rose to prominence as a scene played out before his eyes and then fell into the background again as another took its place. Each of them were different than the one before and it didn't take long for Riley to realize that he was watching events from the past, present, and quite possibly the future play out in an endless sequence on Uriel's flesh.

Events from his own life, in fact.

Glancing at the expressions on the faces of the men around him, he believed they were seeing memories and events related to them in turn.

When Uriel shrugged his shoulders, setting his robe back into place, there wasn't a man left in the room, Green included, who didn't believe the angel was who he said he was.

By now, it seemed, they were all ready to hear what the angel had to say.

"Gabrielle Williams speaks the truth. The Adversary was not destroyed; far from it. He twisted the ancient ritual to his own purposes, releasing the spirits of his former angelic companions into the bodies of the Seven who came to face him, corrupting them from the inside out. He now inhabits the body of the man you once knew as Sean Ferguson, who was, in fact, the angel Lenestiel."

With that revelation, Riley began to understand just what had been happening within the Order. The Adversary, in the guise of Seneschal Ferguson, had been intentionally working to destabilize the Order, destroying it from within.

"But why?" Gabrielle asked. "What is he trying to do?"

Uriel crossed the room to stand before her and gently placed his hands on either side of Gabrielle's face, tilting her head upward so that his eyes were staring directly into hers. She made no move to stop him.

"Here is what the future holds," he said softly and then the ground seemed to fall out beneath her and Gabrielle felt herself falling backward, her body picking up speed as it tumbled away into the darkness.

CHAPTER 34

S HE OPENED HER MOUTH TO scream...

...and found herself standing on a stony point high above the earth, looking down at a highway that cut its way through the rock-strewn landscape far below like a stretch of black ribbon. She wasn't alone; the tattooed man stood beside her, dressed in jeans but bare from the waist up. The tattoos drew her attention but try as she might she couldn't quite understand exactly what she was seeing within their shifting shapes.

She stepped closer, trying to get a better look, but her companion interrupted her perusal by reaching out, grasping her upper arm, and stepping off the edge, taking her along with him.

A sickening sensation of falling washed over her but it stopped as suddenly as it had started. Instead of slamming into the earth at the foot of the cliff, body broken on the unyielding rocks below, she found that she was standing in the midst of a jungle clearing, her companion by her side. Around them was a massive crowd of people, most likely numbering in the *thousands, standing at the base of a stone step-pyramid that carved its way upward toward the night sky above. The sound of drums – many, many drums – came from somewhere nearby, the air literally vibrating with their heavy beat.*

A ceremony was taking place high above on the top of the pyramid. Even as Gabrielle looked on, two burly men wearing feathered jaguar masks brought a woman to the edge of the pyramid, facing the crowd below and forced her to her knees. While they held her arm stretched out to either side, a third man stepped up behind and grabbed her hair, pulling her head up to expose her throat. A knife flashed, one quick, sharp slash across the woman's throat and blood began to spurt outward in long, wet streams, painting the steps below.

The guards shoved the dying woman's body forward, watching as it tumbled end over end toward the screaming crowd below before moving out of the way as another prisoner was brought forward and forced to his knees.

Her companion touched her arm and in the blink of an eye they left the jungle sacrifice behind and found themselves atop a massive dune in the midst of a desert. Africa most likely, *she thought, given the fact that she was currently sitting astride a camel the likes of which she'd only seen in movies or zoos. Her companion rode a similar beast.*

As with their last destination, they were not alone. A group of desert nomads dressed in loose-fitting robes designed to shield them from the desert sun surrounding them. Oddly enough, none seemed to notice the two strangers within their midst; it was as if their gaze slipped right over them whenever one turned in their direction.

Gabrielle turned her attention to what it was she'd been brought to see.

A giant stone statue, easily five stories high, was being constructed in the valley below. Groups of men wearing little more than loincloths in the scorching desert heat were dragging massive stone blocks by hand along the valley floor toward the worksite where others would take over the chore of dragging them up long, earth ramps to their intended position and slotting them into place as part of the statue's form. It was brutal work, made all the more so by what were clearly slave drivers scattered throughout the work crews, driving the slaves onward with the repeated lash of a whip whenever they faltered or slowed their pace.

Gabrielle could almost have imagined that it was a scene out of ancient Egypt, if it weren't for the wreckage of modern vehicles lying half-buried in the drifting sand..

No, this is present day, *she thought,* or pretty damn close to it.

The realization chilled her to the bone.

She was looking about, searching for something that might tell her where she was or who these people might be when the scene dissolved for the third time and she and her companion were whisked away once more.

This time their destination needed no explanation, for Gabrielle immediately recognized the iconic New York skyline. Or, at least, what was left of it. She stood on the top floor of a partially destroyed skyscraper, looking down upon the wreckage of a city laid to waste by what seemed like years of warfare. At first it appeared that nothing remained amidst the ruins, but then her companion raised his arm and pointed, directing her attention to a motorcade that emerged into view.

Gabrielle counted five cars in all; two SUVS in front, a limousine in the center, with two more SUVS bringing up the rear.

The target will be in the center car, *she thought, and was still wondering where such a thought had come from when everything went the hell right there in front of her.*

A rocket raced out of the ruins, striking the lead vehicle smack in the middle of the chassis and exploding on impact, sending it ten feet into the air before it crashed back down in a burning heap. Gabrielle was still gaping in astonishment when a second rocket raced out of the debris, turning the last vehicle into twisted, burning wreckage much like the first. The remaining vehicles were now effectively boxed in between the building debris on either side of the road and the disabled vehicles to the front and rear.

Men dressed in dark BDUs emerged from either side of the road at that point, firing automatic weapons at the two remaining SUVs, ignoring the limousine in the middle.

Recognizing the danger that they were in, the driver of the lead vehicle tried to make a break for it, stomping on the gas and sending his own SUV racing forward, hoping to ram the disabled one in front of him and move it out of the way. His actions backfired, however, as the attackers focused their firepower in his direction, riddling the SUV he was driving with a cavalcade of bullets and killing all those inside.

The men in the final SUV chose to stand their ground and fight back, spilling out of the vehicle and taking cover wherever they could find it. There were too few of them, however, and the resulting firefight didn't last long.

With the bodyguards dead, the attackers advanced on the limousine.

Gabrielle had no idea who was inside, or what they were fighting over. She glanced over at her companion, looking for some insight, but he must have misunderstood her for he simply shook his head and pointed into the distance.

She turned, looking in the direction that he'd indicated, and was just in time to see what she first took to be a flock of birds emerge from behind the hulk of a partially-damaged skyscraper.

But as the birds drew closer...

"Those aren't birds," she said aloud, surprised that she could even hear herself over the roar of the automatic weapons still going off below them.

She didn't know what the hell they were - Gargoyles? Demons? Something worse? – but she could see that they were scaled, reptilian creatures the size of horses supported on bat-like wings as they swooped through the air with the grace of beings one-fourth their size. Within seconds the flock spotted the conflagration going on below, and as one, wheeled about and dove downward, their clawed feet extended like those of a hawk preparing to break the back of its prey.

A shout rose up from the men below as one of their own spotted the diving creatures as well, but by then it was too late. The gargoyles-demons-whatever-the-hell-they-were were among them in seconds, their claws rending and tearing flesh with wild abandon and the attack that had been going so well just seconds before devolved into a rout. Those that survived the initial onslaught scattered like mice, racing into the closer confines of the crumbling ruins around them, hoping to find shelter from the aerial attacks that had decimated their numbers so quickly.

Gabrielle never saw what happened to them, for again she was whisked away to another location, this time in London, and then Sydney, and to Moscow, and lastly, to a barren snow-swept landscape that she instinctively knew was Antarctica. Seven locations. Seven continents. Seven scenes of murder and mayhem.

It was the future of the world under the leadership of the Adversary and his princes.

It was hell.

Uriel let go of her face and Gabrielle stumbled backward, her senses spinning as the things she had seen flowed across the surface of her mind like water bursting from a crack in a pressure dam.

"Now do you understand?" Uriel asked in a booming voice, directed not just at her but at all of the knights assembled in the room.

Glancing around and seeing the expressions on their faces, she realized that somehow Uriel had shown them all the same images, that the scenes had been playing out in their minds even as they were unfolding in her own.

"The Adversary must be stopped or all you have seen will come to pass."

Riley couldn't keep the look of horror off his face. It was perhaps the biggest mission the Templar Order had ever faced and, thanks to the Adversary's machinations, there weren't more than a few dozen of them left to carry it out.

He felt despair begin to overwhelm him.

Riley knew he was a good soldier, a good leader, but he was also enough of a pragmatist to realize that a task like this was beyond his abilities. They needed someone with tactical experience, yes, but also the kind of magnetic charisma that would get other men to follow him to hell and back in order to see things through.

Gabrielle asked the question before he could.

"Where is Cade?"

The archangel glanced at Riley, as if sensing the self-doubt that was festering across the surface of his mind, before turning his attention back to Gabrielle.

"The Nephilim is following his own path."

Nephilim? Riley thought. *What in holy hell?*

Gabrielle either didn't pick up on the significance of the appellation or simply didn't care, barreling right past it.

"Don't give me that crap! I've come all this way and I intend to find my husband. Where is he?"

Uriel considered her a moment and then nodded once, as if acknowledging her need to find an answer.

In an oddly-gentle voice for someone with his power, he said, "Your husband blames himself for your death. He believes that he failed you, not once, but thrice; when the Adversary first invaded your home, when your soul was offered as payment for Cade's ability to bridge the way between worlds, and when he failed to protect you from the Necromancer's ritual. He has dedicated himself to fighting spectres in the Beyond until he either destroys them all or dies in the attempt."

As Gabrielle stared at him in horror, Uriel went on. "Unfortunately, without your husband, this little resistance you've formed has very little chance of succeeding."

CHAPTER 35

RILEY FOUND HIS VOICE FIRST.

"So what do we do?" he asked.

"I would think that was obvious," Uriel answered. "Someone is going to have to enter the Beyond and find him."

That was about the last thing Riley expectedto hear. He had a deep, innate distaste for that other worldly place and he would do just about anything to avoid going back there. Once was more than enough.

An idea suddenly struck him.

"Why don't you go?" he said to Uriel. "You're an archangel, if anyone can find him in that hellhole it would be you."

But their new ally – if they could call him that – was already shaking his head.

"I cannot enter the Beyond."

"Why not?" Riley asked.

"Because the Beyond is just that – beyond the reach of the heavenly host. If I were to enter it, I would fall, just like

Asherael."

Riley cursed inwardly. "But you can open the way there so one of us can go?"

He wanted to laugh bitterly at his own words; one of them wouldn't do a damn bit of good against the things that lurked on the other side.

Uriel shook his head, however.

"I am no more able to open the way to the Beyond than I am to enter it."

"Then how the hell are we-"

Uriel looked pointedly at Gabrielle.

"Me?" she asked.

The archangel nodded. "You, and you alone, can do it." He explained that her earlier efforts at crossing the Veil, her connection to Cade, and her "unique" as-he-called-it nature all combined to give her the ability to open a way to the Beyond. It wouldn't be easy; but with his guidance she should be able to do it.

If she can't, Riley thought, *we're fucked.*

Gabrielle looked around at the knights standing in silence, watching her.

"Fine. Let's do it."

# # #

Miles away, in his office in the Ravensgate commandery, the Adversary snarled in rage and shattered the desk in front of him with a single blow.

He had been monitoring the exchange between the archangel and his new allies through the link he established with the Templar named Green. His attempt to influence the other renegade knights had been going well enough until the wingless bastard had shown himself. His very presence had made the link more difficult to sustain and the Adversary had been forced to focus solely on listening to what was passing between them, rather than being able to actively force Green to interrupt it.

Now he'd heard enough.

So my old friend, Uriel, thinks he can outsmart me, does he? After all the years of standing on the sidelines he thinks he's going to enter the game in the final hours and take the prize when it is just within my grasp? Think again, you stupid pawn!

The Adverary summoned his power and sent one final command to his pet Templar and then severed the link.

Green might be little more than a pawn himself, but pawns had been known to take down Queens in the past so why not now? Why not indeed?

With that issue taken care of, the Adversary turned his attention to the other. Picking up the telephone, he dialed Grand Master Johannson's private extension. The former preceptor picked up on the first ring.

"Yes, Lord?"

"Riley and the rest of the renegade knights are holed up in the offices of an abandoned granite quarry outside of Fairfield. I want you to send our troops to eliminate them immediately."

"Of course."

In his guise as Seneschal Ferguson, he'd urged Johannson to move against the Grand Master and assume his position. The minute the ambitious little Templar had done so, his "friend," the Seneschal, had made several moves of his own, including corrupting the former Preceptor with a conqueror worm of his own. From there, the infestation of the regular Templar ranks had begun. Almost two-thirds of the Order was now under his direct control and it wouldn't be long before the rest were, as well.

With the Templars eliminated from the equation, it would be much easier for his plans for conquest to move forward at an accelerated pace.

So far everything was working to plan.

Well, almost everything, he thought. *There was still the issue of the elusive Nephilim named Williams.*

If Uriel was telling the truth, Williams had been in the Beyond for several weeks now. That was more than enough time for the nature of the Beyond to work on the angelic side of the man's nature, corrupting it from within. For all the Adversary knew, Williams might have already Fallen, leaving no need to send anyone after him.

But Williams had been known to get himself out of some very tight spots in the past.

Best to be certain.

Hanging up the phone, the Adversary moved to the middle of the room, giving himself enough space for what he intended to do. Calling forth his power he summoned a full sneak of shadow demons, thirteen in all. He embedded an image of the former Knight Commander Williams in the feral mind of each of the creatures and sent them on their way.

Thinking he had all of the bases now covered, the Adversary returned to his desk and went back to looking over the maps he'd been examining earlier.

Conquest is a glorious thing, he thought, *one made all the more special when the enemy doesn't know that your coming.*

# # #

No sooner had Gabrielle agreed to make the attempt to rescue Cade than Sergeant Green went berserk. Riley watched in stunned amazement as Green drew his sword, let out a bellow fit for a Viking, and charged across the short distance that separated him from where Uriel stood with Gabrielle.

At first Riley thought Uriel was the target and so he was a bit slow to respond, fully confident that the archangel could defend itself. It was only when he realized that Green had his gaze, and his fury, locked onto Gabrielle that he realized his mistake.

Without Gabrielle, their plan to rescue Cade was over before it began.

Riley fumbled for his pistol, knowing he was already too late.

A shot rang out, looming large like thunder, and Riley looked up to see Gabrielle standing in front of the archangel as if to protect him, a pistol in hand.

Green, thrown over backward by the close-quarters shot, twitched once and went still.

Chaos erupted.

Men began shouting, weapons were raised, and it all might have gone to hell right then and there if Uriel hadn't stepped in. He opened his mouth and literally roared, sending a wave of sound so loud and so powerful washing over them that it was all they could do to cover their ears and pray for it to end.

When the shout died away, Uriel pointed to Green's corpse and said, "Look!"

Green had fallen face-up, the shot that had killed him looking like a third eye in the center of his forehead. As Gabrielle, Riley, and the rest of the Templars looked on, a large, slug-creature as fat around as Riley's fist forced its way out of the bullet hole, trailing a line of blood and brains behind it.

As the creature reached the floor and began moving across it toward the entrance, Uriel grabbed Riley's sword from his hand and cut the thing in half with a single blow. There was a flash of blue light and then the thing laid still.

Gabrielle stared at it with revulsion and then turned to Uriel.

"Tell me that's not-"

"A conqueror worm?" Uriel shook his head. "I can't, because we both know that it is."

Feeling strangely ignorant, Riley asked, "What the heck is a conqueror worm?"

"A psychic parasite," the archangel answered, as he poked the slug with the blade of Riley's sword. Whenever he touched it with the blessed weapon it sizzled like steak on the grill.

Gabrielle continued the explanation, as she bent to pick up Green's sword. "They're harvested from the Sea of Sorrows in the Beyond and can be used on living, to bend them to the harvester's will."

"So someone was controlling Green?"

She nodded, a grim expression on her face. "And most likely listening to everything we were saying as they did so."

There was really only one individual who had both access to the Beyond and a desire to know what was going on within Riley's group of renegade Templars.

The Adversary.

"God in heaven," Riley whispered, resisting the urge to cross himself, then giving into it.

CHAPTER 36

BELIEVING THAT THE ADVERSARY WOULD do everything in its power to prevent them from sending Gabrielle into the Beyond in search of Cade, Riley immediately ordered the Templars to begin preparing to defend their current location against what could only be an imminent assault, leaving Gabrielle to work with Uriel in the hopes of opening a way into the Beyond.

Discarded pallets and large rock carts were strategically placed to allow the defenders shelter against incoming fire. Weapons and ammunition were distributed and stacked within easy reach. He put his two best snipers on the roof and ordered several more men to form an advance position by arranging the vehicles into a defensive position a half-dozen yards in front of the main doors.

After that, there wasn't much to do but wait.

It didn't take long. Within ten minutes of their taking up positions, the first of the enemy showed up at the mouth of the dirt road leading back to the highway. Four SUVS, each carrying half-a-dozen men, pulled to a stop angled in opposite directions across the road, blocking the only way out.

Or so they thought.

Riley knew better. Cade had selected this place and he never would have done anything so stupid as to choose a location with only one way in and one way out. Beneath the building in which they stood was an underground tunnel via which the finished granite blocks had been moved half-a-mile east to a platform where they were loaded onto a train. The train tracks themselves were long since defunct, but Riley had been down in the tunnel not a month earlier and knew it was still functional. As soon as Gabrielle was away, he and his men would retreat in that direction, escaping to fight another day.

For now, he'd let the enemy think they had them cornered.

#   #   #

On the far side of the warehouse, Gabrielle stood with Uriel, preparing to return to the one place she swore she'd never go again.

The Beyond.

She didn't care that she was breaking her vow; all she wanted to do was to find Cade and bring him home. She'd worry about the Adversary and all the rest once she'd managed that much.

"So how do I do this?" she asked.

Uriel shrugged.

It was not the answer she was expecting.

"What the heck does that mean?"

"It means I cannot tell you how to breach the barrier. Only you can do that."

"But back there…" she began, pointing to where the group

had been discussing the situation just moments before.

Uriel cut her off.

"Back there was for their benefit. Would you have agreed to try if I told you I didn't know how to open the way?"

"Of course not!"

The archangel smiled.

"So how the hell am I supposed to do this?"

"How did you do it before?"

"I haven't got a clue!"

"Yes, you do. Your memories are intact; with a little effort they are all there for the taking. See yourself opening the Veil, just as you did when you stopped your husband from killing the Necromancer in New Orleans."

New Orleans? God but that felt like years distant from where she was now.

She closed her eyes and tried to remember where she had been moments before turning up in that desiccated chapel behind the plantation the Circle of Nine had used as their base of operations.

The moment she tried to focus on one memory, however, her mind was flooded with a thousand other thoughts.

Fear for her husband's life.

Anger at the Adversary.

Curiosity about the archangel standing by her side.

Worry about the violence to come.

Dismay that she wouldn't be able to do this.

Damn it, Williams! Knock it off!

But the more she tried, the worse it got.

She was just about to say as much to Uriel when the firing started.

# # #

"Here they come!" Riley shouted to the men around him as several newly arrived SUVS swerved around those that had been parked at the entrance to the complex and raced toward where the Templar commander was hunkered down with his men behind their own vehicles.

The snipers on the rooftop got off the first few shots, but Riley and those around him weren't too far behind. Bullets slammed into the oncoming vehicles with deadly precision in a fusillade of fire that would have pulverized any ordinary vehicle.

These were Templar assault vehicles, however, reinforced with armored plating around the chassis and fitted with bulletproof windows. The gunfire Riley and his team threw at them damaged the vehicles and wounded some of those inside, but didn't stop them completely. Recognizing that the drivers intended to ram their defensive position, Riley ordered his men to fall back inside the building. He waited until the other vehicles were almost upon them and then triggered the explosives they'd packed into the front few vehicles, watching as the blast lifted the oncoming SUVs and slammed them back down again, leaving nothing but broken, twisted wreckage in their wake.

Satisfied they'd given as well as they'd taken, Riley slipped inside the building and rejoined his men to wait for the next wave of attackers.

# # #

"Stop trying so hard. Just see the portal there in front of you and make it a reality."

Gabrielle wanted to scream in frustration. Gunfire and explosions were going on around her – *people where dying for heaven's sake!* – and Uriel kept telling her that all she had to do was relax and focus.

A powerful blast shook the very foundations of the building and Gabrielle was thrown forward. She would have slammed her head against a nearby stack of crates if Uriel hadn't reached out and caught her.

"We're running out of time," he said.

Thanks for the pep talk.

She pulled free of his grasp, walked a few feet away to give herself some room, and did what she could to block out everything around her. She focused solely on her breathing, an old mindfulness routine she'd learned in her youth, in and out, in and out, closing her eyes and just letting everything else drift away.

When she was ready, she began to imagine the portal there before her, the shimmering mirror-like opening that would lead her from this world to the next. She tried to visualize it down to the finest detail, from the silver-green color to the slight ripples that washed across its surface.

A grunt from Uriel reached her and when she opened her eyes, the portal was shimmering there in the air before her.

She'd done it!

She had no real idea how she'd managed it, but that didn't matter. All that mattered was that she'd succeeded!

Then another blast shook the warehouse.

# # #

"Watch out! There trying to flank us!"

Riley felt like the fighting had been going on forever, though he knew it had only been a few minutes. But in that time he and his men had been forced to give up half of the ground they controlled and it wouldn't be long before the mass of troops ahead of them took the rest.

There were just too many of them for his men to hold off for long.

At first, it had been the horror of firing on men you knew, men you'd worked with day in and day out, that had caused them to lose ground they shouldn't have lost. There wasn't anything Riley could do if the men under his command tried to avoid killing their former comrades.

Not that those attacking them had any such qualms, he thought bitterly. It was as if the newly arrived Templars didn't remember that they'd ever been on the same side; they charged his teams' positions with ruthless abandon, throwing away their lives in an effort to overrun the rebels. First his team given up the external ground, then the area around the front door, and finally the middle of the warehouse.

This was it; they had nowhere else to go. They either held this ground long enough for Gabrielle to step through the portal or they'd lose before the real war ever began.

Riley fired a burst from the assault rifle in his hands and then felt it run dry. He had already used the last of his magazines so he tossed the rifle aside and pulled out his pistol. An enemy soldier stuck his head out past the stack of pallets he was hiding behind and Riley drilled it with a snapshot that sent the man tumbling backward where gunfire from several other sources made his now-lifeless body twist and shake.

A cry from behind Riley caught his attention and he turned

to see the gleaming shape of a portal burst into existence at the back of the warehouse.

Gabrielle did it!

\# \# \#

"Remember, time passes differently in the Beyond," Uriel shouted over the din of the gunfire around them. "Find Cade and return as quickly as you can. We'll be waiting for you!"

Gabrielle nodded, grabbed the sword she'd taken from Green, and then hurried over to the portal. Taking a deep breath, she lifted one leg and stepped across the opening, feeling the power of the doorway pulling at her, wanting to drag her from this world into the next. As she gave into it, she chanced a look back.

She could see Riley standing in the gap between their hastily-assembled fortifications, firing at the incoming soldiers who were spreading out across the warehouse floor. He was doing everything he could to buy her a final few, precious seconds to make the passage across the Veil. As the portal pulled her into its depths, she saw an enemy grenade bounce across the floor to land at Riley's feet.

"No!" she shouted.

The Templar leader tried to throw himself out of the way, but it was too late.

The last thing Gabrielle saw was Riley's body being lifted into the air by the concussive blast of the explosion and then the darkness of the Beyond claimed her as its own and she knew no more.

The story continues in DARKNESS REIGNS (Coming Spring 2016)

Made in the USA
Lexington, KY
27 December 2016